W9-DID-539

"Date a lot of single moms, do you?"

"Not so far." Heath regarded Claire steadily. "What about you? Dating anybody?"

"No."

He let his gaze rove over her hair, face and lips. "Why not?"

"I'm running a business meant for three all by myself," she said. "It's in the red. I'm bringing up the twins all by myself, and in case you haven't noticed, they're a handful."

His expressive lips tilted up in a playful half smile. "A cute handful. They have to sleep sometime."

Their gazes meshed and the seconds drew out. His head bent. Hers tilted. Their lips drew ever closer.

He was going to kiss her.

And she was going to let him!

Dear Reader,

We all have our doubts. My husband and I always have a hard time deciding what car to buy. Trying to decide where to vacation is easier. And we have no doubts at all about our decision to marry and live the rest of our lives together.

Claire Olander knows she can make the Red Sage Guest Ranch & Retreat a success. She worries about being a good parent. Sure, Heidi and Henry love her and enjoy being with her. But does she really have what it takes to help the four-year-old twins get past their parents' deaths? Is her love for them going to be enough to guide her?

Heath McPherson is a whiz at handling trusts. When it comes to money, he concentrates on the bottom line. Then he meets Claire, and the twins, and the decisions he has to make are suddenly driven by more than numbers. Which causes him to wonder—does he have what it takes to be professional in a situation where he gets more and more emotionally involved with the trust beneficiaries (aka the twins) and their beautiful guardian (Claire) every day? Is he going to be able to do his job *without* losing the woman and children he loves so much?

I hope you enjoy reading this story as much as I enjoyed writing it.

Happy reading!

Cathy Gillen Thacker
THE INHERITED TWINS

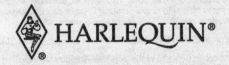

HARLEQUIN®

TORONTO • NEW YORK • LONDON
AMSTERDAM • PARIS • SYDNEY • HAMBURG
STOCKHOLM • ATHENS • TOKYO • MILAN • MADRID
PRAGUE • WARSAW • BUDAPEST • AUCKLAND

ISBN-13: 978-0-373-75235-5
ISBN-10:   0-373-75235-0

THE INHERITED TWINS

ABOUT THE AUTHOR

Cathy Gillen Thacker is married and a mother of three. She and her husband spent eighteen years in Texas, and now reside in North Carolina. Her mysteries, romantic comedies and heartwarming family stories have made numerous appearances on bestseller lists, but her best reward, she says, is knowing one of her books made someone's day a little brighter. A popular Harlequin Books author for many years, she loves telling passionate stories with happy endings, and thinks nothing beats a good romance and a hot cup of tea! You can visit Cathy's Web site at www.cathygillenthacker.com for more information on her upcoming and previously published books, recipes and a list of her favorite things.

Books by Cathy Gillen Thacker

HARLEQUIN AMERICAN ROMANCE

997—THE VIRGIN'S SECRET MARRIAGE*
1013—THE SECRET WEDDING WISH*
1022—THE SECRET SEDUCTION*
1029—PLAIN JANE'S SECRET LIFE*
1054—HER SECRET VALENTINE*
1080—THE ULTIMATE TEXAS BACHELOR**
1096—SANTA'S TEXAS LULLABY**
1112—A TEXAS WEDDING VOW**
1125—BLAME IT ON TEXAS**
1141—A LARAMIE, TEXAS CHRISTMAS**
1157—FROM TEXAS, WITH LOVE**
1169—THE RANCHER NEXT DOOR†
1181—THE RANCHER'S FAMILY THANKSGIVING†
1189—THE RANCHER'S CHRISTMAS BABY†
1201—THE GENTLEMAN RANCHER†
1218—HANNAH'S BABY††

*The Brides of Holly Springs
**The McCabes: Next Generation
†Texas Legacies: The Carrigans
††Made in Texas

Chapter One

In most situations, twenty-nine-year-old Claire Olander had no problem standing her ground.

The only two Texans who could weaken her resolve ambled to a halt in front of her. In perfect synchronization, the "negotiators" turned their faces upward.

Her niece, Heidi, pushed the halo of short, baby-fine blond curls from her face and tucked her favorite baby doll under her arm, football-style, so the head faced front. "How come we have to clean up our toys now, Aunt Claire?" the preschooler demanded.

Her twin brother, Henry, adjusted his plastic yellow hard hat with one hand, then gave the small wooden bench he was "fixing" another twist with his toy wrench. His amber eyes darkened in protest as he pointed out with customary logic, "It's not dinnertime!"

Claire wished it was. Then the business meeting she had been dreading ever since the bank auditors left to tally their results, six weeks ago, would be history. Aware there was no use worrying her nearly four-year-old charges, she smiled and tidied the stacks of papers on her desk one last time.

Everything was going to be all right. She had to keep

remembering that. Just like her late sister, Liz-Beth, she was more than capable of mothering the twins and managing the family business they'd started. "We are cleaning up early, kiddos, because we have company coming this afternoon," she announced cheerfully. In fact, the Big Bad Wolf should be here at two o'clock.

Heidi sat down cross-legged on the floor, placed her doll, Sissy, carefully across her lap, and began stuffing building blocks ever so slowly into a plastic storage bin. "Who?"

Claire knelt down next to her, and began to help, albeit at a much quicker pace. "A man from the bank."

"Can he hammer stuff?" Henry demanded.

Claire surveyed the two children who were now hers to bring up, and shrugged. "I have no idea."

Heidi paused. "What *can* he do?" she asked, curiously.

"Manage a trust." *Destroy my hopes and dreams...*

Henry carefully fitted his wrench in the tool belt snapped around his waist, and sat down beside Heidi. "What's a trust?"

"The fund that's going to pay for your college education one day."

"Oh." He looked disappointed that it wasn't something he could "repair" with his tools.

"Is he our friend?" Heidi asked.

Claire fastened the lid on the building blocks bin, and put it on the shelf in her office reserved for the twins' playthings. "I've never met him, honey. He just moved here a couple of weeks ago." She'd heard a lot about him, though. The newest member of the Summit, Texas, business community was supposed to be thirty-three years old, to-die-for handsome and single, a fact that had the marriage-minded females in the community buzzing. Fortunately for Claire, she was not one of the group jockeying for attention. She had her hands full with her fledgling business and the twins she had inherited from her late sister and brother-in-law.

"Is he going to have good manners?" Henry, who'd lately become obsessed with what to do and what *not* to do, inquired.

"I'm sure Mr. H. R. McPherson is very polite," Claire said. Most bankers were.

Heidi put Sissy on her shoulder and gently patted her back, as if burping her. Her brow furrowed. "What's H. R. McDonald's?"

"H. R. McPherson, honey, and those are initials that stand for his first and middle names." Claire could not blame him for using them on business correspondence, even if it did make him sound a little like a human-resources department. "Although," she observed wryly, shelving the last of the toy train cars scattered about, "who would name their son Heathcliff *and* Rhett in this day and age, I don't know."

"As it happens," a low male voice drawled from the open doorway behind her, "the hopeless romantic who came up with that idea was my mother."

As the sexy voice filled the room, it was all Claire could do to suppress her embarrassment. Talk about bad timing! She'd just mouthed off about the man she could least afford to insult.

Slowly, she turned to face the interloper.

The ladies in town were right, she noted with an inward sigh. Tall, dark and handsome did not begin to do this man justice. He had to be at least six foot four inches tall, and buff the way guys who worked out regularly were. Nicely dressed, too, in a striking charcoal-gray business suit, navy-and-gray-striped shirt and sophisticated tie.

His midnight-blue eyes glimmering with amusement, he waited for her to say something.

Flushing, Claire flashed a smile. "This is awkward," she said.

"No kidding."

She took in the chiseled features beneath the thick black hair, the straight nose, the eminently kissable lips. "And you're early."

He shrugged and stepped closer, inundating her with the compelling mixture of soap, man and sun-drenched November air. "I wasn't sure how long it would take me to find the ranch." He extended his hand for the obligatory greeting, then assisted her to her feet. A tingle of awareness swept through her.

"I didn't think you'd mind," he added cordially.

Claire probably wouldn't have, had she not been down on the floor with the kids, speculating inappropriately about his lineage, at the exact moment he'd walked in.

Ever so slowly, he released her hand, and she felt her palm slide across the callused warmth of his. She stepped back, aware she was tingling all over from the press of skin to skin.

"You can call me Heath," he told her.

She swallowed nervously. "I'm Claire." Aware of the little ones taking refuge at her sides, she cupped her hands around their shoulders and drew them closer, conveying that they would always be safe with her. "And this is Heidi and Henry, the beneficiaries of the trust."

Heath shook their hands solemnly. "Pleased to meet you, Heidi. Henry, nice to meet you also."

"Pleased ta meet you!" the twins echoed, on cue.

Claire grinned, happy her lessons on manners were sinking in.

"So when do you want to get started?" Heath asked in a more businesslike tone.

"Just as soon as their sitter arrives," Claire declared, glad he was putting them on more solid ground.

FORTUNATELY FOR HEATH, that wasn't long in coming. A pickup truck parked in front of the office and a petite woman, with cropped salt-and-pepper hair, got out. Claire introduced Mae Lefman, who, with a warm smile, led the children out of the office.

Through the double hung windows that fronted the ranch office, Heath watched them go. "Nice place you've got here," he remarked.

He knew, of course, that the Red Sage Guest Ranch and Retreat had been in the Olander family for several generations, and that oil had been drawn from the ground, until the wells all went dry.

Claire's dad had dabbled in ranching and worked to restore the property to its natural state. Claire and her late sister and brother-in-law had figured out yet another way to earn a living from the twenty-nine-thousand-acre spread.

Which was why he was here.

Heath braced himself for what could be a very unpleasant meeting. Tensing visibly, Claire Olander gathered the flowing folds of her chiffon skirt close to her slender legs and sat down behind her desk. She wore a dark-green turtleneck sweater, the same hue as the floral pattern in her skirt, and a charcoal-gray corduroy blazer. Soft leather boots peeked out from beneath the hem of her skirt.

Her hair was the same wildly curly honey-blond as her niece's and nephew's, the shoulder-length strands pulled back from her face in a clip on the back of her head. Silver feather earrings adorned her ears.

She was a fair bit shorter than he was, even with the three-inch heels on the boots—maybe five foot seven. Slender. Feminine. Sexy in an innocent, angelic way. She was also stubborn. He could see it in the feisty set of her chin and the determined look in her long-lashed amber eyes.

Claire Olander was used to having things her own way.

And that, Heath knew, could be a problem.

He sank into a chair opposite her. "As you know, I've been recently assigned by the bank to administer the trust your sister and her husband left for the twins."

"Right. The banker who was doing it retired from First Star Bank of Texas a few weeks ago."

Heath nodded. "As trustee, my duty is to protect the financial interests of the kids. I'm concerned. The results of the audit were not good."

This was, Heath noted, no surprise to Claire Olander. She held up a slender hand. "I'm aware the health of the business could be better, but I've only had the guest cottages up and running for the past eight months."

He had noted how shiny and new everything looked when he drove in. "Orrin Webb, my boss at the bank, told me you opened after the death of Liz-Beth and Sven."

With sadness flooding her face, Claire turned her attention to the scenery outside the window. "This was our dream. Neither of us wanted to sell the ranch. Nor were we interested in trying to run cattle here, the way our dad did."

"It's my understanding that you inherited all the surface improvements on the property—meaning the ranch house and the barn—and your sister was bequeathed the mineral rights."

"The latter of which are worth nothing, since the wells here were pumped dry forty years ago."

"The land is owned jointly and can only be sold in one piece, if all parties agree."

"That's correct."

Heath consulted his notes. "You and your sister had equal shares in the guest-ranch business."

Again Claire nodded.

"Heidi and Henry received all their parents' assets upon their death, all of which remain in trust."

"That's correct."

Heath looked up again, as determined to do his job as she was to do hers. "Wherein lies the problem. The trust needs to be generating—not losing—income. The results of the annual audit in September show that the business is in the red."

"Some months it's in the red, others it's in the black. For instance, we were fully booked most of June, July and half of August."

Heath had known she was going to be difficult. "What about now?" he pressed.

Her shoulders stiffened. "What do you mean?"

"How many of the twelve guest cottages are rented?"

Claire flushed. "Thanksgiving is two weeks away."

"That doesn't answer my question."

She let out an aggravated breath and shot him a challenging look that in no way detracted from her femininity. "Right now, we have three of the cottages rented. Mr. and Mrs. Finglestein from upstate New York are here for two weeks. They're avid birders. Ginger Haedrick is here until the house she is building is ready to move into—that may not be until Thanksgiving week, though she'd like to get in sooner and is pushing the builder along. It might work—Ginger is one of the real-estate brokers in the area."

"I've met her." She seemed ambitious, almost ruthlessly so. "She came by the bank to give me her business card, and offered to find me a place to live as soon as my townhome in Fort Stockton sells."

"And then we have T. S. Sturgeon, the mystery writer, who's here on deadline, trying to finish a book. I think she'll be at least a few more weeks, but again, it all depends."

"Which means you have a quarter of the cottages rented," he stated.

"It's *off-season.*"

"How are the bookings for the holidays?"

Claire Olander pursed her incredibly soft-looking lips. "Does it matter? It seems you've already made up your mind that the Red Sage Guest Ranch and Retreat is a failure."

"I didn't say that."

Eyes flashing, she took a deep, bolstering breath. "Your questions implied it."

Silence thrummed between them.

"Here's the bottom line." Heath tried again. "If nine months pass and the trust is not productive—not turning a profit—something must be done. The mineral rights could be sold, for example."

"No!" She cut him off, her voice unexpectedly sharp.

"Or a portion of the business."

"Absolutely not!" She vaulted to her feet.

Heath stood, too. He put his notes away. "Look, I'm aware this is a lot to digest. You've got two weeks to think about it. In any case, on December first, the Tuesday after Thanksgiving, I am going to have to make some changes."

"What if I can get the bookings up and demonstrate that the business will start turning a profit immediately? Would that change things?"

Heath nodded. "Definitely. The trust doesn't have to be making a large profit, Claire. Particularly if there is potential for a lot of growth in the long run. There just has to be some."

She shrugged and planted both hands on her slim hips. "Well, then, I'll make it happen."

Trying hard not to notice how the preemptive action had drawn her sweater and blazer against her breasts, Heath said, "Speaking of vacancies… What would you think about me renting one of the cabins for the next few weeks?"

Claire froze, regarding him suspiciously. "The ranch is a twenty-five-minute drive from town."

Heath told himself he was not doing this to help her out financially. Nor was he doing it because she was treating him in a way that young and beautiful women never did. "I don't mind the commute," he told her with a challenging grin. And he liked the peace and quiet of the ranch. Liked the backdrop of rough granite and wild meadows, the mountainous backpacking terrain. This, he thought, was southwest Texas at its best.

He'd only been out here half an hour and he could see why she was so determined to hang on to her inheritance.

She studied him impassively. "When did you want to move in?"

"Tonight."

To her credit, she didn't so much as blink. Rather, she reached into her desk and removed a rental contract, plucked a pen from the holder on her desk and pushed both toward him. "How long do you want to stay?"

"Until my place in Fort Stockton sells and I find one here."

This time, he noted, she did blink. "So we're talking…"

"Weeks. Possibly months."

She paused. Whether she was happy about his request or wary, he couldn't tell. "I assume we're talking about a one-bedroom cottage?" she said finally.

He matched her pragmatic tone. "Yes."

Claire told him what the rate would be.

"Sounds fine."

After she made a copy of his credit card, she took a map of the ranch and a thick ring of keys from her desk. "You can have Cabin 1, which is closest to the ranch house, or Cabin 8."

"I'll take the closest one to the ranch house," Heath said without hesitation.

Claire led the way out of the office. Together, they walked across the gravel parking area, past a big red barn, to the path that led to the dozen cottages. The rustically designed structures were spaced well apart and attractively landscaped with native grasses and shrubs. The November air was brisk and clean, the red sage the guest ranch was named after in full bloom.

Claire stopped at the first homestead-style cottage. The one-story building had white clapboard sides, red shutters and door, and a sloping slate-gray roof. She unlocked the door and gestured him to enter. "As you can see, the unit has a small sitting room and a galley kitchen. The bedroom has a queen-size bed. Thermostat is here." She pointed to the wall, then the closet. "Extra linens are there. Cabins are made up once a week, unless you want to pay for daily maid service."

"Once a week is fine."

"There is a complimentary breakfast buffet every morning in the front parlor of the ranch house." Claire pressed the key into his hand and glided toward the front door.

Heath followed, surprised how sorry he was to see her go. "Dinner—?"

She flashed a regretful smile. "—is not currently offered."

"How DID IT GO?" Orrin Webb asked.

Heath bypassed his own office, heading for the branch manager's. Orrin was very old-school, from his salt-and-pepper crew cut, to the horn-rimmed glasses he wore. He exuded a by-the-book attitude, mirrored by his starched white, button-down shirt and dark suit.

Shrugging, Heath sank into a chair opposite his boss's desk. "About as well as could be expected, given the news I had to deliver."

Orrin rocked back in his chair and propped his fingertips together. "I take it she's resisting any easy fixes?"

"Like selling off part of the business? Yeah."

"You don't need her permission to do anything in regard to the trust," Orrin reminded him.

"The success of the bank depends on the continued goodwill of people in the community. If they think we're steamrolling over her and the kids, just to increase the bottom line, they won't be bringing their property to us to put in trust. They'll let someone else see to the fiscal welfare of their heirs."

The other banker smiled. "And here I thought you might have trouble getting the hang of life in a smaller town."

"Summit may only have five hundred people but there are ten thousand more in the surrounding county. I want all their business coming here."

"My thoughts exactly. So what are your plans?"

"First, get to know Claire Olander and acquaint myself with the guest-ranch business she and my clients own. See if it really has the potential for growth that she thinks it does." Because if it didn't, Heath knew, he was going to have to sell the twins' share, even if he had to do it over her objections.

"How are you going to do that?"

"By staying at the Red Sage until my place in Fort Stockton sells."

"She agreed to let you?" his boss asked.

"She needs the cottages rented. At the moment, the majority of them are vacant."

"Did you talk to her about Wiley Higgins?"

"She wasn't in a frame of mind to hear it."

"He's not going to wait long before he pursues his goal," Orrin warned.

"Well, he better wait a while. 'Cause I'm telling you, if he goes in there too soon, his chances of success are nil."

Orrin paused. "What do you think your chances are of getting Claire Olander to see things your way?"

That his intervention could, Heath thought, be the answer to all her prayers? "At the moment? Slim to none."

Chapter Two

Heath had just driven up and parked when Claire came out of the ranch office late that afternoon. She walked straight toward him. "I had a call from someone named Wiley Higgins today. He wants to see me about a business matter and he used you and the bank as a reference."

It was all Heath could do not to grimace. "I didn't know he intended to phone you today."

Claire's eyes narrowed. "What does this guy want? Aside from a cottage to rent from now until after Thanksgiving?"

Heath nodded at the dusty truck making its way up the lane. "Why don't you ask him yourself?"

As Wiley parked his pickup, then climbed down, Claire eyed the name and logo painted on the side: Higgins Oil Exploration.

She tensed, just as Heath figured she would.

The young wildcatter wore a turquoise Western shirt, mud-stained jeans and expensive alligator boots. He swept off his black Resistol, held it against his chest and extended his other hand. "Claire Olander?"

She shook hands with him, her reluctance to have anything to do with oil companies reflected in her wary expression. "Mr. Higgins, I presume," she murmured dryly.

"You said on the phone you had a cottage I could rent."

She nodded. "And you said you had a business proposition you wanted to discuss with me."

"If it's all the same to you, ma'am—" Wiley shoved his cowboy hat back on top of his tangled, dishwater-blond hair "—I'd rather do that over dinner this evening. Soon as I have a chance to get cleaned up. Maybe the two of us could go back into town?"

A wave of unexpected jealousy flowed through Heath. He frowned.

Claire shook her head. "That's not going to be possible. I have two little ones to feed."

As if on cue, Henry and Heidi walked out of the ranch office. "We're hungry, Aunt Claire!" her nephew announced.

"We're going to have dinner as soon as I take care of Mr. Higgins and show him where he is going to be staying."

Undeterred, Wiley suggested, "I could join the three of you."

Why couldn't the oilman get the message to back off? Heath wondered. He turned toward the interloper, his shoulder brushing Claire's in the process. "The ranch doesn't serve dinner," he interjected mildly.

"I'd be happy to pay extra," Wiley declared.

So would Heath, as it happened. And not just because it would be convenient.

Claire looked at him. He shrugged and said, "Serving dinner would be a way to increase income for the ranch on a daily basis. I'd be in."

"We'll make it worth your while," Wiley offered. "Twenty-five dollars for each of us. You can't say no to an extra fifty bucks."

Claire looked as if she just might. "You don't even know what we're having for dinner tonight," she protested.

The wildcatter straightened the brim of his hat. "Doesn't matter, so long as it's hot and home cooked."

Heath hadn't had a home-cooked meal since he'd moved from Fort Stockton and lost access to a full kitchen. "Got to agree with him there," he said.

"Fine. But just so you fellas know, it's a one-time-only proposition," Claire said. She handed Wiley the paperwork for his cabin and a key. "I'll meet you in the ranch house kitchen at six-thirty. Henry, Heidi, come on, we've got work to do."

HEATH HAD JUST FINISHED shaving and brushing his teeth when the cottage phone rang.

Claire was on the other end of the line. "Would you mind coming over about ten minutes early? I've got something I'd like to discuss with you."

"Be right there." Whistling, Heath crossed the yard. Thanks to the recent switch from daylight saving time, it was already dark. The lights of the sprawling ranch house shone warm and welcoming. The smells coming from the kitchen were even better.

The twins were seated at the kitchen table, busy with coloring books and crayons. They each had a small bowl of dry cereal and a glass of milk nearby—probably to take the edge off their hunger while they waited for whatever it was that smelled so good to finish cooking.

"Hi, kids." Heath took in their angelic faces and thought about the lack of family in his life, how much he wanted to have a wife and kids of his own and a home just like this to come to every night.... He'd had his chance, of course, but it hadn't worked out. Now all he had were his regrets.

"Hi, Mr. Fearsome." It was Heidi who spoke, but both twins beamed.

"McPherson," Claire corrected.

"Mr. Fearsome," the little girl repeated, enunciating carefully.

Heath grinned. "Close enough. Need a hand?" he asked Claire.

"What I need to know..." she paused to taste the applesauce simmering on the stove "...is what's going on between you and Wiley Higgins."

Reluctantly, Heath moved his gaze from her soft, kissable lips to the fire in her eyes. "What do you mean?"

She added another sprinkle of cinnamon and a pinch of nutmeg to the aromatic compote. Deliberately, she set the spoon on its rest, wiped her hands on a tea towel. "I saw the two of you exchanging words in the yard before you entered your cottages."

Heath waited.

She propped her hands on her slender waist. "I have the feeling I'm at the center of the disagreement."

Hoping to spare the twins any unnecessary worry or alarm, Heath kept his gaze on Claire's and inched closer. "Then you would be right."

Her eyes darkened. "Why?"

He shrugged. "Wiley Higgins can be dogged in his quest for something."

"So in other words, you feel you need to protect me from his single-mindedness."

Unused to being penalized for taking charge of a business

situation, Heath said, "Not protect." If ever a woman seemed capable of standing on her own, it was Claire Olander.

"Then what would you call it?" she asked.

He gestured enigmatically. "Doing things in an orderly fashion."

She'd taken off the blazer she had been wearing earlier. Now she pushed the sleeves of her sweater to her elbows. "And how would we do that?"

Heath tried not to notice the smooth, pale skin of her forearms as he braced one hip against the counter. "We'd start by sitting down together and taking a detailed look at ways to improve your guest-ranch business."

She turned so that one of her hips was resting against the edge of the counter, too. "I've already done that," she snapped.

He maintained an even tone as he replied, "You haven't shared any of the ideas with me."

"Fine." Claire released an exasperated breath that lifted the swell of her breasts beneath the soft fabric of her sweater. "When did you want to do this?"

He shifted restlessly, to ease the building tension behind his fly. "As soon as possible." He wanted time to implement changes.

As Claire considered her options, she gave the simmering applesauce another stir. "The car pool picks the twins up at eight-thirty tomorrow morning. I can do it any time after that."

"Eight-thirty it is, then," Heath agreed promptly.

Wiley Higgins swaggered in just then, freshly showered and shaved. He looked from Claire to Heath and back again, then he smiled like a detective who had just found an interesting clue. "What'd I miss?"

CLAIRE WASN'T SURE whether she resented or welcomed the interruption. All she knew for certain was that Heath McPherson had the ability to get under her skin with surprising speed.

Working around him was not going to be easy. Either in this kitchen, where his imposing frame took up way too much space, or in business, when it came to satisfying the fiscal requirements of the trust. But she would manage—she had no choice.

"Have a seat, fellas." Claire took the roasting pan from the oven. She moved the already sliced pork tenderloin to a platter, and spooned roasted potatoes, green beans and applesauce into serving dishes. After placing them on the table, she brought out a tossed green salad from the fridge.

"Henry, do you want to try the pork tonight?" she asked.

When he shook his head, she popped two slices of whole wheat bread into the toaster and got out a jar of peanut butter.

Heidi explained solemnly, "Henry only eats peanut butter toast for dinner."

"Really?" Wiley said. "This food looks awfully good."

"I'll eat it," Heidi interjected proudly. "I like everything. But Henry doesn't."

Her brother glanced at Heath. Claire, too, was curious to see the man's reaction.

"I'm glad you know what works for you," he said. "It's important for a fellow to know his own mind."

Henry's eyes widened appreciatively. That was not the reaction he usually got.

Claire flashed Heath a grateful smile, then sat down at the table. While they helped themselves, family-style, to the food, she cut straight to the chase with Wiley. "So what was this business you wanted to discuss with me?"

"I'm in Summit County to look for oil."

She lifted her palm. "The wells on the Red Sage went dry forty years ago."

That information didn't deter Wiley. "Conventional extraction yields only thirty percent. The rest of the oil squeezes into tiny cracks in a reservoir and clings to the underground rocks. There's a process now that wasn't available at the time your wells were capped, called water-flooding."

"I know all about injection wells," Claire said. Out of the corner of her eye, she saw Heath accept a bite of Heidi's green beans with great relish. Suppressing an amused smile, she continued, "The oil companies push water into the ground and try to wash out the remaining oil."

Wiley nodded, as Henry offered Heath a bite of peanut butter toast. "That'll get out a portion, but not all. Adding surfactant could get out even more."

Claire shook her head, as Heath offered Henry a bite of his meat, which he refused. "I don't want chemicals on my land," she said.

Ignoring the increased restlessness of the kids, Wiley pushed on. "We could also inject steam or carbon dioxide into the wells."

Henry offered Heath another bite of peanut butter toast, which was wordlessly accepted. Not to be outdone, Heidi gave him another green bean.

With effort, Claire pushed aside thoughts of how comfortable he was with the kids and what a great dad Heath would be, and brought her mind back to the business at hand. "Injecting steam requires putting in huge pressure vessels to heat the water. I don't want anything that dangerous or noisy or intrusive on the ranch," she stated decisively. "The same goes for carbon dioxide."

"How about putting microbes into the wells then?"

It was all she could do not to roll her eyes. "Microbes produce large amounts of gas and pressure underground."

"Properly handled," Wiley countered, with the smoothness of a snake oil salesman, "that shouldn't be a problem."

Claire disagreed. "It's bacteria. We have well water out here. I'm not taking any chances that our drinking water might be contaminated, now or in the future."

Heath gave her an admiring glance. "You know a lot about this."

Glad for the interruption, she nodded. She wanted him to understand her position. "A couple years before my dad died, after he had stopped running cattle out here, an oilman came by and tried to convince him to reopen the wells. Dad said it took him forty years to get the land back to its natural state. No way was he letting heavy trucks and machinery tear up the place, after all his hard work."

Wiley cleaned his plate. "There could be a lot of money involved here, Claire."

About that, she noted in disappointment, Heath did not disagree. But then, what had she expected? He was a banker— a bottom-line guy.

"And it could be," she countered, "that the process of getting to whatever oil is left in there—if there is any in the ground on this ranch—is not going to be economically viable for you or any other wildcatter."

Wiley frowned. "Don't you want to find out?"

She scowled right back. "Nope."

And then and there, the twins' patience—what was left of it—ended.

Henry tipped his milk glass over. Heidi did the same. The liquid from Henry's flowed into Wiley's lap, that from Heidi's splashed onto Claire's. Both victims sucked in a distressed breath as Heath, who'd been unscathed, grabbed for napkins.

"Oh my goodness!" Claire jumped up to get clean dish towels to mop them up.

Wiley grimaced as the liquid soaked into his pants. He looked as uncomfortable as she felt. "No problem," he drawled. "Accidents happen."

Only, Claire thought, it hadn't been an accident.

"EVERYTHING OKAY?" Heath asked twenty minutes later, when Claire finally came back downstairs, this time without her two young charges.

"The twins are fine." She sighed, feeling a lot more comfortable now in faded jeans and a loose-fitting shirt. "Just overtired." She'd scolded them gently for their end-of-dinner behavior, then helped them brush their teeth and change, and finally tucked them into bed.

The effort left her feeling the way she did every night around this time—like she had just run a marathon.

Claire paused to look around. "What happened to Wiley?"

"He took his pecan pie à la mode and went back to his cottage to change and check his messages."

Before sprinting up the stairs with the twins, Claire had told the guys to help themselves to dessert and coffee. Heath had apparently not yet done so, in favor of cleaning up the table and scrubbing the pots and pans. She studied his rolled-up shirtsleeves, and the damp towel thrown across one broad shoulder. He looked as at home in her kitchen as she was. She wouldn't have expected that of a man in his line of work.

She watched the play of muscles in his brawny forearms as he scrubbed down the table and counters with an enticing combination of strength and finesse. She edged closer, taking in the brisk woodsy fragrance of his cologne. "You didn't have to stay." But she was suddenly glad he had. It was nice having company—attractive male company—after hours.

Finished with the cleanup, he let the sudsy water out of the farmhouse-style sink. "I felt I owed you after such a delicious meal."

Claire reminded herself Heath was a paying guest. And as such, not a target for lusty fantasies.

Pushing away the image of those same nimble fingers on her bare skin, she quipped, "And a rather inglorious end."

He chuckled. "Tip things over accidentally-on-purpose often, do they?"

"No." Thank heavens.

Heath hung up the dish towel and lounged against the counter again, one palm flattened on the gleaming top. "I get why they did that to Wiley. He's a bit of a blowhard. But why they doused you—now that's a mystery."

Claire shook her head ruefully. "I think they were trying to tell me I should have paid more attention to them during the meal. Suppertime is their time. They get my undivided attention. I should have known better than to turn it into a business meeting and a chance to pick up some extra cash, by charging you two for the meal."

Heath's blue eyes narrowed. "Why did you?" he asked with curiosity.

She sighed. "I knew I had to hear Wiley out sometime, or risk him pestering me to death. I figured the twins' brief attention span would keep his sales pitch short, and I would have skated by, without offending a paying guest. Which, you may have noticed," she intoned dryly, "I need."

"And me?"

Easy, Claire thought, cutting them each a slice of pie. "I wanted you to know my opinion on what he is trying to do, and it was easier to have you hear it firsthand than for me to repeat it."

"Ah." Heath watched her scoop out the vanilla ice cream.

Their hands brushed as she handed him a plate and fork. "So now that you do—"

"That's it?" Heath interrupted, taking a seat at the kitchen table again. "I don't get a chance to weigh in? As trustee?"

Claire sat opposite him. "Not tonight." She marveled at how much this was beginning to feel like a date.

He shrugged, even as he savored his first bite of pecan pie. "Fair enough."

That, Claire thought, was a surprise. She had expected him to be just as pushy as Wiley Higgins, when it came to business. Yet he was giving her a pass, at least for now. To get on her good side? "So back to the dishes. Thank you for doing them."

"No problem."

"But in the future, it's not necessary." Claire resisted the intimacy his actions engendered. "You're a guest here. Not the help."

A brooding look came into his eyes. He spoke in a kind, matter-of-fact voice. "I was raised by a single mom. I remember how tired she was at the end of every day. So I helped then. And I help now, whenever I see a woman in need of assistance."

A poignant silence fell between them. Was that how he saw her? Claire wondered. She deflected the rawness of the moment with a joke. "Date a lot of single moms, do you?"

"Not so far." Heath regarded Claire steadily. "What about you? Dating anybody?"

She flushed. "No. Not for the past couple of years."

Appearing just as distracted as she was, Heath let his gaze rove over her hair, face and lips before returning with laser accuracy to her eyes. "Why not?"

"I'm running a struggling business meant for three all by myself," Claire reminded him. "I'm bringing up the twins on my own, and in case you haven't noticed, they're a handful."

His expressive lips tilted up in a playful half smile. "A cute handful." He stood and carried his empty plate to the dishwasher.

Claire did the same. "They take every ounce of emotional energy I have, and then some."

"They have to sleep sometime."

"And generally, when they do, I do. Seriously, I was never so tired before I became their mom. My sister always made it look so easy." Claire sighed, wishing Heath didn't have a good eight or nine inches on her in height. The disparity in their bodies made him seem all that more overwhelming.

He clamped a gentle hand on her shoulder. "It probably was, comparatively, if there were two parents handling things."

Tingling beneath his grip, Claire stepped back. "So what are you saying?" she demanded, raising her hands in a mock gesture of helplessness. "I should get married? Go husband hunting?"

"Wouldn't hurt to open the door to the possibility," he told her wryly.

Aware that her pulse had picked up, Claire conceded, "Maybe in five, ten, fifteen years, when they go off to college. Until then, I'm on my own and staying that way."

"Sure about that?" he murmured.

Claire straightened with as much dignity as she could manage. "Quite sure."

He smiled. Their gazes meshed and the seconds ticked by. His head bent, and hers tilted upward. Their lips drew ever closer. He was going to kiss her, Claire realized suddenly, and she was going to let him!

Or at least he would have kissed her just then, had it not been for the pitter-patter of little feet just outside the kitchen door.

The adults turned in unison as Heidi and Henry entered the room. As always, they looked adorable in their pajamas, their blond curls askew.

Heidi had her favorite doll baby, Sissy, tucked beneath her arm again. "Aunt Claire?" she asked, her expression absolutely intent.

Claire's heartbeat quickened even more. "Yes, honey?"

"When are Mommy and Daddy coming home?"

Chapter Three

Claire breathed in sharply, clearly thrown off guard by the twins' innocent query. Briefly, a mixture of grief and shock crossed her face.

Just as quickly, she pulled herself together and approached the twins. Kneeling down in front of them, she wrapped her arms about their waists, and pulled them toward her. "Mommy and Daddy are in heaven," she said very gently. "Remember? We talked about this."

"Yeah," Heidi said, pointing upward as if to demonstrate her comprehension. "But heaven's up there in the sky."

"And birds are, too," Henry concurred.

"But birds come down. On the ground. So when are Mommy and Daddy going to come down on the ground, too, and come see us again?" Heidi asked plaintively.

"We miss 'em," Henry said sadly.

"I know you do," Claire said, her own voice thick with unshed tears. "I miss them, too. But they can't come back and be with us, as much as we want them to."

Heidi and Henry fell silent, their expressions both stoic and perplexed. Claire gave them another hug. "What do you say we go upstairs and I read you another story?"

"Can he come, too?" Henry pointed at Heath.

"Yeah. I bet he likes stories," Heidi declared.

"We can't ask Mr. McPherson to do that," Claire said softly.

The twins both looked as if they were about to pitch a fit.

Figuring a change of mood was in order, Heath interjected, "Sure, I can. In fact, I've got to tell you, I am one fine story-reader. I can even do voices."

Claire sent Heath a grateful look, making him glad he had intervened.

Heidi's brow furrowed. "What do you mean, you do voices?"

"Ah!" Heath held out a hand to Henry, who looked the most ready to revolt. "I guess I'll have to show you. What stories do you like best?"

"Ones about Bob the Builder," Henry said, thrusting out his bottom lip.

"Ones about dolls," Heidi declared. "And Sissy likes them, too."

Together, they all headed through the hallway, past the formal rooms, reserved for ranch guests, and up the wide front staircase. Claire looked over their heads and mouthed, "Thank you," to Heath.

He whispered back, "You're welcome."

Twenty minutes and four stories later, the twins were finally drowsy. "It's bedtime now, for real," Claire said. "You have preschool tomorrow morning, and you don't want to be too tired to enjoy it."

"Okay." Henry stifled a yawn, holding out his arms for a hug. Claire obliged. When she released him, Henry turned to Heath, and held out his arms again.

Ignoring the sudden lump in his throat, Heath hugged the little boy. At times like this, he wished he had made better choices. If he had, he might have married a woman who wanted children as much as he did. Instead, he was still searching for a woman who wanted the same things out of life. A woman who yearned for more than a successful husband and a growing bank account. A woman who would put family first. A woman like Claire. And kids like the twins.

Heidi hugged both of them, too, then smothered a yawn with the back of her hand, too. Clasping her doll Sissy, she snuggled down into the covers. "Night," she said, already closing her eyes.

Heath's heart filled with tenderness.

"I'll see you in the morning." Claire backed out of the room, Heath following suit. Soundlessly, the two of them crept down the stairs.

They walked back to the kitchen. "Do you want some coffee? I can't drink regular this late in the evening, but I can handle decaf," she told him.

"Sounds fine. Thanks."

Claire released a breath. "You were great just now."

Seeing how upset she still was, wanting to help in whatever way he could, Heath leaned in the doorway. "Does that happen often?"

"Once every couple of weeks now. Initially, it was all the time." Claire's hands trembled as she tried to fit the paper filter into the coffeemaker. Eyes focused on her task, she continued, "The psychologist our pediatrician referred us to said that children under age eight don't really grasp the concept of death. They don't understand the finality of it. So it takes them a long time to really accept and adjust to the fact that their loved ones aren't coming back, that they won't see them again on this earth." Claire raked her teeth across her lower lip, shrugged her shoulders helplessly. "I've tried to explain about heaven, about how one day we'll all be together again, but I don't think they get that, either."

Without warning, the tears she had been holding back splashed down her cheeks.

Heath didn't have to think; he knew what he had to do. He crossed the kitchen in two long strides and took her into his arms. No sooner had he pulled her against his chest than the dam broke. Claire's whole body shook with silent sobs. His shirt soaked up her tears, and still she cried, her face pressed against his shoulder. He wrapped his arms closer around her, not sure what to say, only knowing that she needed to be held as much as he needed to hold her. Finally, the shuddering stopped.

Claire wiped the heel of her hand beneath her eyes, then drew back. "I'm sorry," she sniffed.

"Don't be."

She shook her head, looking aggrieved. "I shouldn't be behaving this way. Especially not with you…"

Heath stroked a hand through her hair. "You've got every right to be sad," he soothed. But even as he spoke, he could see she didn't want to feel that way. She wanted the mourning to be over. She wanted to be able to move on.

And he wanted to help her do that.

CLAIRE SAW THE KISS coming. Realized she could stop it. All it would take was a look, a sigh, a shake of her head. Instead, she lifted her face to his and stepped back into his embrace. Her lips parted as his touched hers, and then everything in her life that was painful and wrong, everything that should never have happened, faded away.

She reveled in the taste and smell of him, in the tenderness of his touch and the reckless abandon of his kiss. He held her as if she were the most fragile possession on earth. He kissed her as if she were the strongest. And in truth she felt both.

Like she could handle anything.

She just didn't want to handle it alone.

Not anymore.

And that, more than anything, was why she broke off the kiss and stepped back.

They faced each other, their breathing erratic.

But the apology she half expected from Heath never came.

And it was easy to see why.

Judging from his expression, he wasn't sorry he kissed her. Any more than she was that he had. And what was up with that? She knew better than to mix business with pleasure, to get involved with a paying guest. And she especially shouldn't be kissing the man in charge of the twins' trust fund. Which was why she had to get him out of here before they got any closer.

She flashed an officious smile and glided away from him. "Let me get you a cup of coffee for the walk back to your cottage."

"Thanks."

She filled a mug, turned and handed it to him. Their hands brushed once again as the transfer was made, and Claire felt another whisper of desire float through her, stronger than before.

Until now, she hadn't realized how lonely she was.

Now, she knew.

And so did he.

"See you in the morning," he said.

"Eight-thirty," she confirmed, her heart still pounding, all her senses in overdrive.

But, as it happened, she saw him sooner than that. Heath was in the front parlor, helping himself at the breakfast buffet, when she shepherded the kids toward the front door, to wait for their preschool car pool. He was clad in a navy-and-white pin-striped shirt and navy suit that made the most of his tall, muscled frame and brought out the blue of his eyes. One look at his ruggedly handsome face and enticing smile and she knew he was thinking about the kiss they'd shared, as much as she was.

Deliberately, Claire turned away. "Now, remember," she told the twins, as she stopped at the front hall closet and took a gift-wrapped package off the shelf. "You're going to a birthday party this afternoon. Buddy Nesbitt's mommy and daddy are going to drive everybody to Buddy's house, and you're going to have pizza and birthday cake, and play games. And then when the party is over, I'm going to come and get you and drive you home."

"Are they going to have candles?" Henry asked, standing patiently as Claire helped him into his light jacket.

"Yes. I'm sure they'll have candles on Buddy's cake."

"Is he going to do that wish thing and blow them out?" Heidi asked.

"Yes, he gets to make a wish, and then he blows the candles out."

"But he can't tell anybody or it won't come true," Heidi recollected solemnly.

"Right. Birthday wishes are secret," Claire said.

"I want a birthday," Henry declared.

"Your birthdays are coming up next week."

Heidi perked up. "Do we get a party?"

"You do," Claire said. "It's going to be at the park and you can invite all your friends. It should be a lot of fun."

"Yes!" Henry clapped his hands together.

Hearing a car rumbling up the drive, Claire opened the door and herded the kids out to the nine-passenger vehicle. She handed the present to the mom driving the car, for safe-keeping, made sure the twins were both buckled in, then stood waving as the van disappeared again.

Heath came out to stand beside her. "The twins seem okay this morning," he noted.

Remembering how much help he had been to her the night before, she turned to him with a wry smile. "That's the way it is. One minute they're confused and grieving, the next it's like nothing ever happened."

Heath searched her eyes. "I gather you have a harder time bouncing back?"

"Unfortunately, I understand the finality of our loss." As an image of her late sister came to mind, Claire swallowed. She focused her attention on the horizon as she confessed, "I think the holidays are going to be tough."

Sympathy radiated in his low voice. "Your first…"

She nodded. "Without Liz-Beth and Sven, yes." She swallowed again, then knotted her hands into determined fists at her sides. "But we'll get through it, because we still have a lot to be thankful for." She paused, drew a bolstering breath. "Speaking of which, you ready to go over to the ranch office and talk about how we can make the numbers work?"

He nodded, all business once again. "Lead the way."

HEATH SETTLED IN A CHAIR on the other side of Claire's desk, aware this wasn't an ordinary business meeting, any more than the kiss they'd shared the night before had been ordinary. What happened in the next few weeks would either make or break Claire's dreams for the Red Sage, while simultaneously securing the twins' inheritance.

Heath did not want to be in the position to make that kind of impact on her hopes for the future. But it was his job. And he always did his job.

Claire folded her hands together and consulted the handwritten notes in front of her. "You said the other day that as long as the business demonstrated the potential for growth, as long as the guest ranch could turn a small profit, you wouldn't have to sell anything."

Trying not to notice how pretty she looked in a dark-gold sweater and brown-and-gold paisley skirt, Heath nodded. "The problem is, according to the rates you've set for the rooms, that's not going to happen, with the kind of occupancy you've got right now."

She leaned back in her swivel chair. "We were at capacity for seven weeks this summer."

Heath kept his eyes locked on hers. "And not even half occupied since September."

A delicate flush highlighted her cheeks. "I put up a Web site, and that's bringing in some business. But obviously I've got to do more, which is why I've written to every newspaper and magazine editor in the state and let them know we're open for quiet R & R, family reunions, business retreats."

"When did you do that?"

Resentment colored her tone. "I started sending out letters the end of August, the beginning of September, when things slowed down."

A good move, but possibly not enough. "What's the response been?" Heath asked.

The evasive look was back in her eyes. She started to rise. "Can I get you some coffee?"

He respected her too much to be anything less than forthright. He shook his head in answer to her question and said, "It's not enough just to send out brochures."

She sank back in her desk chair and rocked back and forth impatiently. "I've made phone calls, too."

"Any results?"

She hedged. "All it would take is one good review in *Southwestern Living* magazine, or the travel section of a Houston or Dallas paper travel section, and I'd be fully booked in no time."

"Even if you were to get good press right now, I'm afraid it might be too little too late."

Claire massaged the back of her neck with both hands. "If we could just hang on until next spring, and be patient…"

Heath pretended not to notice the way her posture drew his attention to her curves. "Right now the ranch is operating anywhere from five hundred dollars a month in the black to five thousand dollars in the red."

"I know." Claire dropped her hands. A pleading note came into her voice. "But if you average those numbers over the nine months we've been open, I'm only short a thousand a month."

He wished he could cut her a break. "What about the winter months coming up?" he inquired matter-of-factly. "Do you have bookings?"

Again she looked regretful. "Some."

"How many?"

Claire sighed. "Not enough."

Not nearly enough, he thought in disappointment, when she reluctantly showed him her list of reservations. "Is there any other way you can bring in money?"

She tilted her head and the subtle movement brought him the lavender scent of her perfume. "We had plans to turn the barn into a party facility, use it for wedding receptions and big parties, but Sven and Liz-Beth died before we could get started on that."

It was a good idea. Unfortunately, it couldn't happen fast enough. "You could charge for breakfast."

Claire disagreed. "All the big hotel chains offer free breakfast with an overnight stay now. To stay competitive, I have to do that, too."

Silence fell as they both stared at the numbers on the pages in front of them. "Is there any equipment you could sell—like a tractor or something—to temporarily add to the profits?"

"We liquefied everything we could when we were building the cottages. What little lawn we have mowed now, that isn't xeriscaped or returned to the wild, is done by a rancher in the area." Claire leaned forward, and Heath sensed it was all she could do not to grip his hands. "If I can get good press, more exposure, I can turn this around."

Heath figured he could ask around at the bank, see if anyone at the other branches had any ideas, or was in a position to call in a favor. In the meantime, he would be straight with her. "You've got a little less than two weeks."

Claire was unable to mask her disappointment. "And if I can't manage to turn things around by then?" she asked warily.

He exhaled, hating to be the bearer of bad news to such a sweet woman. "Then we're going to have to look at doing one of two things. Lease or sell at least part of the mineral rights to the ranch. Or sell off part—or all—of the twins' share of the business."

If he had to do either, Heath knew, she would end up resenting the heck out of him.

There'd be no more kisses.

No more confidences.

Not even the possibility of romance.

And that really stunk.

IT WAS NEARLY EIGHT in the evening by the time Heath left the bank, grabbed a bite to eat and got back to the Red Sage. As he pulled into the parking lot, real-estate broker Ginger Haedrick drew up beside him. They got out of their vehicles at the same time.

Ginger gestured toward the office, where lights were blazing. "What's going on?"

Through the windows, Heath could see most of the other Red Sage guests milling around Claire. "I don't know. Let's find out."

The two of them went over to the office.

When they walked in, Heidi and Henry looked up from the toy corner. They had obviously already had their baths, and were in their pajamas.

"Hey!" Henry's face lit up. He elbowed his sister. "Look! It's Mr. Fearsome."

Heidi grinned, too. She plucked a picture book off the shelf and ran over to him. "Can you read us another story with voices?"

"We went to a party today," Henry declared, ignoring his twin. "They had cake and everything."

"Yeah." Heidi clutched her storybook to her chest, and peered up at Heath. "We helped Buddy blow out the candles because he couldn't do it all by himself."

"That's great." Heath smiled.

Ginger looked over at the banquet table in the corner. It was covered with a gingham tablecloth as well as boxes of pizza, paper plates and napkins. An ice-filled washtub holding canned sodas sat on the floor next to it. "Y'all having a party?" she asked, in a tone that indicated if it were true, it wasn't much of a celebration.

"We're helping Claire make a sales video for the ranch," Mr. Finglestein said. He and his wife were dressed identically in khaki trousers, plaid shirts and multipocketed canvas vests. Both had binoculars slung around their necks. The excitement in their eyes made them look younger than their fifty-something years.

Mrs. Finglestein nodded and indicated the jumble of cameras, cables and laptops connected to Claire's computer. "We're letting Claire use some of the footage we've shot while we've been birding."

T. S. Sturgeon, the mystery writer on deadline, looked up from the yellow legal pad she was scribbling on. "I'm writing the copy." She paused and considered Heath. "You have a nice voice. Deep. Resonant. Quietly authoritative. Maybe you should do some of the voice-overs."

Mrs. Finglestein nodded. "It would be worth your while. If you help, you get a free night's stay."

Claire avoided Heath's eyes. With good reason, he thought. Making the sales video was a good idea, but reducing her profits for the month even further by giving away free lodging was not.

"Ginger could give it a try, too," T.S. said. "Maybe have both a man and a woman speaking."

Mrs. Finglestein nodded. "Might broaden the appeal."

The twins tugged on Heath's pant legs, soundlessly pleading for him to pick them up. Aware they were a little old for that, but also probably a little overwhelmed by the chaotic activity, he scooped one up in each arm.

"Read to us!" Heidi tried to give him the book, and ended up thunking him in the chin.

Claire sent them a distressed look. "Kids…!"

The door to the office opened. Mae Lefman, babysitter and part-time ranch employee, walked in.

Claire's spine relaxed in relief.

"I got here as soon as I could," Mae said, with a smile.

"They're all ready for bed," Claire told her. She crossed over to the children, and one by one, removed them from Heath's arms, kissing and hugging them before setting them down next to Mae.

"I have work to do." Claire knelt and faced Heidi and Henry, meeting them on their level. "So Mrs. Lefman is going to put you to bed and stay there with you until I'm finished."

"Can Mr. Fearsome read us a story with voices?"

"No, honey, not tonight. But Mrs. Lefman will read to you."

"How about Curious George books?" Mae suggested, holding out a hand to each twin. "They're lots of fun."

Wistfully, Heath watched the children walk across the yard to the ranch house. It shouldn't matter to him who read the kids a bedtime story. But somehow it did…

Which probably meant he was getting way too involved.

"So how about it?" T.S. asked, drawing Heath back to the present. "Either of you interested in doing the voice-overs?"

"Thanks for the invitation, but Heath and I already have plans," Ginger interjected. "I promised to show him some real-estate listings this evening so we can start looking at properties tomorrow. Maybe we can help some other time?"

"Don't worry about it." Claire looked at Ginger with the patience of a saint, given the agent's rather snotty attitude. "But thank you for the offer."

"If you need a voice-over," Heath interjected, "or any other help, count me in. I don't know a lot about putting together a video, but I'm a quick study."

"Thanks. But I think we've got it covered. Y'all should stick to your original plans."

She was jealous, Heath realized with surprise. And there was no reason for her to be. Now was not the time to clear that up, however. That was a discussion best had without an audience. "Well, if you think of anything I can do, let me know," he volunteered. "I'll be back later."

Claire nodded and turned back to the computer screen in front of her.

Clearly resenting anything that got in the way of her making a sale, Ginger touched Heath's elbow and escorted him toward the door. "The house I want to show you hasn't come on the market just yet," she said, loudly enough for everyone else to hear. "But it's renovated and move-in ready. If you like it, we can make a preemptive bid," she added, ignoring the fact he'd told her he did not want to purchase anything until his old home had sold. "You could be moved into your new place before the Thanksgiving holiday...."

And not so coincidentally, Heath thought, off the Red Sage. Away from Claire and the kids....

"PUSHY, ISN'T SHE?" T.S. murmured, after the two had left.

Struggling not to feel resentful, Claire shrugged, "Ginger's just doing her job."

"She's after Heath," Mrs. Finglestein stated.

So what if she was? It wasn't Claire's business. One kiss did not make her and Heath a couple, or anywhere close to it. They hadn't even gone on a date. Nor were they likely to, given their complicated business relationship. "He's single," she said stiffly.

Mr. Finglestein studied her. "*You* should make a play for him," he announced.

Claire flushed. Deep down, she'd had much the same thought. "Why do you say that?"

He shrugged. "I don't know."

"Because you'd make a cute couple!" his wife exclaimed.

"Not everyone needs to be married." T.S. turned to Claire with a wink. "But a little romance is always nice."

Claire's face was now fire-engine red. "He's a guest!" she declared, as if that settled it.

"And you're a woman and he's a man," Mrs. Finglestein quipped. "Seriously. You're both available. We all saw the way Heath was looking at you just now. You should think about pursuing the attraction."

"What's the harm in generating a few sparks?" T.S. teased.

None, Claire thought. Unless her plan to make the guest ranch a success sputtered and failed, and Heath was forced—by virtue of his own responsibilities—to end her family's dreams.

Chapter Four

Figuring he should take advantage of the trails everyone had been raving about, Heath set his alarm, grabbed a flashlight and went for a predawn run. The morning was crisp and clear and the air felt good in his lungs. Coming back to the ranch house afterward, he noticed that the lights were on.

Through the windows, Heath could see Claire moving around the kitchen.

He wondered if she was still ticked off at him, and even more curious as to why it mattered so much. After all, the two of them had just met.

He exhaled.

It all came down to the kiss they'd shared. His response to her, hers to him. There was definitely something there. Some special chemistry he could not ignore. He paused to stretch out his muscles, drew a few more deep, cooling breaths, then sauntered in.

Claire took a pan of freshly baked cinnamon rolls from the oven and set them on the counter to cool.

"Everything okay?" he asked.

She gave the pot of oatmeal a stir. "Why wouldn't it be?"

Damn, but she looked gorgeous in a long denim skirt, a

chestnut-hued sweater and the stack-heeled boots she wore around the ranch. Her honey-blond curls had a mussed, casual look that suited her perfectly. Heath edged closer. "You were up awfully late last night."

Bypassing the coffee simmering on the warmer, she poured him a tall glass of ice water from the pitcher on the counter. "How do you know?"

Heath chugged the liquid gratefully. "I saw the lights."

Her expression closed, she didn't comment.

Okay, so she was ticked off at him. "Did you get your video finished?" he pressed.

"Yes." Seeing he'd finished his water, she poured him some coffee with the impersonal politeness of a restaurant hostess.

Heath studied the pink color in her cheeks. "What's the plan?"

Claire avoided his eyes as she mixed confectioner's sugar, vanilla and milk. "Why are you asking?"

He matched her contentious tone. "Why don't you want to tell me?"

She raised her chin, resentment simmering in her amber eyes. "Perhaps because you don't approve and you don't even know what I'm doing," she blurted.

Heath took a sip of coffee, finding it as delicious as everything else she cooked, which somehow rankled even more. "I didn't say that," he stated evenly.

She released a short, bitter laugh. "Didn't have to. I could see the little cash register in your brain going when you heard I bartered a night's rent in exchange for help making the video."

Heath exhaled. "You have to admit that's not going to improve your cash flow."

"We'll see," she said shortly.

He finished his coffee in silence and set his mug down on the counter. "You don't want to tell me anything more about it?"

She reached for the decanter and refilled his mug. "Nope."

Another silence fell, until Heath finally cleared his throat. "About Ginger…"

Claire tasted the frosting she was making and added a bit more vanilla. She hit the switch on the mixer, keeping her eyes on the concoction swirling around in the bowl. "I really don't want to talk about Ginger, either," she said tightly.

Resisting the urge to forgo all conversation and simply pull her close and kiss her again, he said, "I know how she made it sound last night."

"Really." Claire turned off the mixer and planted a hand on her hip. "And how was that?"

"Like she and I are getting closer than we are."

Claire's brow lifted. "Shouldn't you be having this conversation with her?"

"I don't have to—Ginger knows where she and I stand. Ours is a business relationship, period."

"Yeah, well—" Claire's lower lip shot out "—so is ours, and you kissed me."

Heath tore his gaze from her mouth. "That kiss had nothing to do with business," he told her gruffly.

"I agree." Her eyes glimmered with emotion. "Which is why it shouldn't happen again, given the fact that you and I have a *business* relationship."

"Actually, we don't have a business relationship," Heath corrected, aware that, ethically, there was a fine line, and he was walking it. "My business arrangement is with your niece and nephew."

Claire began icing the rolls. "You represent the fiduciary interests of the kids. And I'm their guardian."

"Which puts us on the same team, because you want what is best for them, too."

The buzzer went off. She slipped on heat-proof gloves and removed a casserole from the oven. "I'm just not sure we agree what that is going to be."

Heath wasn't, either. "I want you to succeed," he said finally.

Noting him eyeing the egg, sausage, cheese and potatoe medley, she went ahead and cut him a square. It was piping hot and delicious, and only helped make her case that she knew what she was doing here....

"Then do whatever you have to with the bank and the trust to give me more time," she pleaded, in a way that made it very hard to resist.

Heath reminded himself to stay in business mode. "I'd like to help you in any way I can."

"But you're not going to, right?" Claire twisted her lips as the phone rang, then reached over and picked it up. "Red Sage Guest Ranch, Claire Olander speaking.... Your parents and their friends stayed at the ranch last summer? I'm sorry. I don't remember, but we were.... I don't normally rent to anyone under twenty-one. I see." She paused. "You understand it's a dry county and we don't allow drinking on the ranch?"

Heath cleaned his plate as the phone conversation continued. Claire gestured for him to help himself to more. She grabbed a piece of paper and pen and began jotting down names and numbers.

"Right now, we have seven cabins available. Three are two bedroom, with a sofa bed in the living room, so they can sleep a maximum of six adults. If you want to do that, I'm going to have to charge you per adult. Tonight? Sure. I can have everything ready by seven-thirty. Cash is fine. Thank you. Yes. See you then."

Heath lifted a brow. It was easy to see something good had happened, from the excited gleam in her eyes.

"We've got twenty-eight college kids checking in tonight," she reported.

The number sounded good. The type of guest did not. "There goes the peace and quiet."

Heath expected her to be insulted. Instead she laughed and went back to icing rolls. "You *are* old."

Heath could not understand why she wasn't concerned. "They'll be up all night," he predicted. Not to mention the damage to the property that might be done.

Claire regarded him confidently. "I don't think so."

He blew out a frustrated breath. "Then you're naive."

She continued to smile as if she'd won the million-dollar lottery. "Are we done calling names here?"

"Who's calling names?" Ginger breezed in the back door. "Any chance I can grab a roll and a cup of coffee for the road?"

"Help yourself."

The real-estate agent plucked one of the unfrosted rolls off the tray, then smiled at Heath. "I'll pick you up at the bank at five tonight?"

"Make it six," he said, wishing she hadn't chosen this moment to remind Claire they were going out to look at property.

Ginger smiled. "Six it is, then." Breakfast in hand, she sashayed toward the door. Reaching it, she turned back and said with deliberate cheer, "Have a great day, y'all."

Claire gave Heath a look that said he had just lost every bit of ground he had gained with her, and then some.

"Oh, I plan to," she said.

CLAIRE MANAGED TO AVOID any direct personal contact with Heath for the next two days. She was busy with the influx of guests, and he was rarely around, despite the fact it was a weekend. Claire told herself she was happy he wasn't there. One less thing to worry about. Obsess over. Yet on Sunday afternoon, as she was stripping cabins of their linens and towels after the group checked out, and she heard Heidi say, "There he is!" her spirits inexplicably rose.

She knew who the twins were talking about even before she turned around.

Looking innocent as could be, Heath sauntered toward them, stopping when the twins barreled into his legs. The two giggled in delight as he swooped them up in his arms simultaneously.

No one had done that since Sven died.

Claire felt tears well up inside her, but she pushed them away. She was *not* going to cry right now…. She took a deep, bolstering breath.

"Did you see all the bi'cles?" Henry asked Heath.

He spared her a quick, assessing glance before turning back to the little boy. "I sure did."

"There were lots and lots of them," Heidi exclaimed.

"We're too little to ride bi'cles," Henry announced.

"Yeah. If we want to ride something, we have to ride our trikes!" Heidi said.

"Want to see us ride our trikes?" Henry asked.

"After we're done," Claire interjected, before they could jump out of Heath's arms and run off to get them. "We're in the process of taking out all the trash and collecting the linens. Remember? Say goodbye to Mr. McPherson, kids, so we can get back to our chores."

Their expressions altered instantly. "Do we hafta?" Henry asked sadly.

Heidi's lower lip shot out petulantly.

Their disappointment affected Heath. "Actually, I'm not doing anything. I could push the cart, too."

"But you're a guest." Claire protested.

Gently, Heath set the twins back down on the ground in front of Cottage 2. He challenged her with a steady. "You accepted help from other guests."

As if it were already settled, Henry walked up to the hotel laundry cart. "We'll show you how to do it. First I gotta fix it with my wrench." He got the plastic tool out of the carpenter's belt around his waist and twisted and tightened the handle. Finished, he stepped back to admire his handiwork, the way he had seen his dad do.

Claire's heart ached for him.

Heidi hugged Sissy close to her chest. Twisting a curly lock of her blond hair around her fingertip, she stared up at Heath as if he were the answer to her prayers.

Deciding it was easier to accept Heath's assistance than explain to the twins why she couldn't, Claire walked back inside the cottage, picked up the bundle of bed and bath linens and dumped them into the cart. The plastic bag of trash went into a second wheeled container.

With Heath "helping," the twins wheeled the cart to the next cottage in need of cleaning.

Claire unlocked the door and ushered the kids inside. "Come in while I collect the linens," she said.

Heath followed. "You were right, and I was wrong," he told her.

She went to one side of the bed, he went to the other. Together, they made short work of stripping off the sheets. Somehow, the action was as intimate as sleeping together. Maybe because of all the forbidden images being in a bedroom with this gorgeous man conjured up....

Sensing Heath was not a man who apologized often, she took the bait. "Wrong how?"

"About the college kids. I've never seen hotel guests that quiet, never mind at that age." He shook his head in wonderment. "How'd you do it?"

Claire smiled smugly. "I promised them ten percent off their tabs if no noise complaints were registered."

"Still, it was a risk…"

"Not really. As soon as I heard they were trying out for the Olympic team, I knew they'd be all about their training. The only thing I had to do was make arrangements at a restaurant in town for their evening meal, according to their strict dietary requirements, and be here to hand out keys and open up the barn so they could store their bikes in there every evening."

"I guess this means you'll make a profit this month."

"Yes, as it matter of fact it does." Not by a whole lot, Claire conceded silently, but enough to move to the plus side of the ledger. Or it would have been, had she not just spent all that money mailing out DVDs to travel editors across the Southwest in hopes of getting some good press. Figuring Heath did not need to know that yet, however, she merely smiled.

"So what are you going to do when you finish this?" he asked.

"Henry and Heidi and I are going to put the sheets in the washing machines, make invitations for their birthday party and take them to the post office."

He slid his fingers in the back pockets of his jeans. "Sounds fun."

"You're going to help with that, too?" Heidi beamed.

Heath looked at Claire, brow raised in silent inquiry, and waited for her response.

FOR A MOMENT, Heath thought Claire was going to brush him off. Then she said, ever so casually, "It's up to Mr. McPherson, kids. He may have to go look at some more houses or something."

Nice dig. Excellent delivery. Heath grinned like the innocent man he was. "I'd love to help with the invitations."

The kids danced around, practically falling over themselves in excitement. "Mine are going to be purple and yellow!" Henry declared, as they walked into the ranch office.

"Mine are all going to be red," Heidi reported as Claire got out the multicolored ink pads and stamp set.

"You don't have to worry about your clothes." Claire looked him over, head to toe, lingering just a millisecond too long on the apex of his jeans before returning, with a telltale flush, to his eyes. "The ink we're going to be using is nontoxic and washes out easily."

"Good to know." Although it wouldn't matter if he got something on himself, since he was dressed in worn jeans and an old shirt.

Heath folded his tall frame into a child-size chair at the wooden table the kids used for crafts.

Looking about as comfortable as he felt in the cramped

quarters, Claire sat opposite him. Their knees bumped beneath the table, giving Heath a momentary sense of warmth.

"What color do you like best?" Henry asked, as Claire passed out the invitations and showed the kids where they could place their stamps.

Heath had to think about that. He didn't really have a favorite color. Or did he?

His gaze still on Claire's face, he said finally, "When it comes to eyes, I like golden-brown the best." As she began to blush, he told the kids in mock seriousness, "Amber is what they call it, I think."

"What color are my eyes?" Heidi propped her fist on her chin.

"Amber," Claire said.

"What are color are mine?" Henry asked.

"They are also amber. As are mine," Claire continued, heading off the question she knew was coming next.

"What color are your eyes?" Heidi asked Heath. She leaned closer.

"What color do you think they are?" He bent down so she could see.

"Blue," she declared.

Heath turned to Henry.

"I think they're blue, too," he stated.

"Then I like blue eyes," Heidi declared, stamping madly.

Heath turned to Claire. "What about you? Do you like blue eyes?"

"On some people," she replied tartly. The challenge in her expression made him laugh.

A moment later, she regarded him wryly. "So how *is* your house hunting going?"

Aware that he had never been less interested in a potential investment, Heath pressed the stamp of a bunny rabbit into a pad of yellow ink. Imitating the kids' artistic style, he decorated the invitation he was working on. They kept surreptitiously checking on his "technique," while he worked just as hard to keep an eye on what they were doing, so he could copy it correctly.

"I've looked at only two houses in Summit so far. A spec house that's about half built, and actually got a bid on it Friday morning, so it's no longer available. That's why Ginger was so insistent I see it when I did. She knew another party was interested. She showed me another one—a resale—Friday evening. It didn't officially go on the market until yesterday, and she wanted me to have first look and a chance to make a bid."

"And?" Claire started stamping pink sailboats.

Heath and Heidi traded invitations and worked on each other's with just as much enthusiasm as they had their own. "It was as great as Ginger said, completely redone inside and out."

"And yet I gather you weren't interested?"

In such situations, Heath relied on his gut feeling. His instinct told him not to commit to any property at the moment. "I'm not even sure where I want to live yet. In town or not. I always thought I'd want to live in the city—or as close to city as we get out here—and not the country. But being on the ranch the last few days has changed my mind." He paused, reflecting. "I like the quiet." And a whole lot more.

CLAIRE LIKED HAVING HEATH here. Too much. "Maybe you should consider looking at a small ranch," she said eventually, ignoring the sexual tension simmering between them.

His eyes lit up. "That's an idea. Although I don't think I want to raise cattle or breed horses."

Claire couldn't contain an impish grin. "You could always put an oil well in your front yard," she teased.

"Funny."

She sighed. "I wish I thought so."

Heath's gaze became protective. "Wiley still bugging you?"

Telling herself Heath's gallantry meant nothing, she said, "I've rarely seen him since he made his pitch at dinner the other night. Mae told me he's been working on all the neighbors, trying to get them to let him prospect on their land."

"Any takers?"

"I haven't heard so." That didn't mean there wouldn't be. Money talked. Big money talked louder. But that wasn't what she wanted to know about. Claire tapped her chin with her index finger. "Come to think of it, I've hardly seen you the last few days, either."

"That's because I've been working overtime at the bank," Heath replied. "I just took over the management of a trust that's extremely complicated, and losing money right and left. I had to restructure it. Figure out which investments had to go, which could stay."

He was so pragmatic.

He must have noticed the tense, uneasy set of her shoulders. "I'm not going to do that to your trust. Any changes that would need to be made would be fairly straightforward. And you know that, because we've already gone over the options."

Unfortunately, the only one Claire really wanted was the one goal she might not be able to make happen.

Bored by the adult conversation, Henry yelled, "We're all

done, Aunt Claire!" To prove it, he stamped the back of his hand and then his wrist.

Heidi grinned and stamped her wrist, too. "Can we mail them now?"

"Yes." Claire went to the Out basket on her desk to collect the preaddressed, stamped envelopes.

"Then can we eat? I'm hungry!" said Henry.

Claire glanced at the clock on the wall. It was almost four! How had it gotten so late? Had she and Heath really been talking that long? Had the kids actually sat still for all that time?

"Let me take you to dinner," he said.

Claire wished she could go out with Heath, and have a real, adults-only date. "I can't," she told him with sincere regret. "I have to drop these off at the post office and then make dinner for the kids."

"They can come."

"Come where?" Henry shouted, at the top of his lungs.

"With us. Into town. To a restaurant. Does that sound good?"

"Yeah!" Heidi bounced up and down in excitement.

Claire took in the twins' ebullient state. "Once again, you don't know what you've signed up for," she told Heath, glad he had done so, anyway.

"Once again, I'm eager to find out."

THEY WENT TO THE Summit post office and mailed the birthday invitations, slipping them through the slot inside the post-office lobby.

Their mission accomplished, they strolled back to Claire's SUV and put the kids in their safety seats.

"Where did you want to go to dinner?" she asked Heath as she turned her red Grand Cherokee onto Main Street.

"You choose the place," he said.

Claire drove past the fast-food restaurant with the new playground. The kids loved going there, but never ended up eating anything—they spent all their time climbing on the indoor gym. They didn't like Asian cuisine. She cooked both Tex-Mex and barbecue regularly. They'd just had pizza the other night. "How about the new family-style steak place across from Callahan's Mercantile & Feed?" She hadn't yet had a chance to try it, but she'd heard it was good and not too expensive. Casual places like that usually had a children's menu. And they could go in their jeans without feeling out of place.

Heath's grin confirmed him to be the meat and potatoes aficionado she had suspected. "Sounds good to me."

It was still early enough for them to be seated right away.

The waiter set crayons and pictures to color in front of the kids, then handed Heath and Claire menus. He took their drink orders and headed off.

Claire turned to the children's selections on the last page. Her expression fell.

"Problem?" Heath asked.

"No *p-e-a-n-u-t b-u-t-t-e-r.*"

"You want to…"

"No." This was as good a time as any to try to get Henry to broaden his horizons again, foodwise. "Henry, Heidi. Let me tell you what your choices are for dinner."

They looked up, listening.

"Macaroni and cheese. Chicken fingers. Hot dogs. Hamburgers. Or sirloin steak."

"Mmm." Heidi had to think about it. "Mac'roni," she said.

"Okay. You're also going to get green beans and applesauce and milk with that."

"Okay." She went back to coloring in earnest.

"Henry, what did you want?" Claire asked.

"Peanut butter toast."

"They don't have that here, honey."

"I eat peanut butter," Henry repeated, in a tone that brooked no negotiation.

Claire could push the issue, of course. If she did, there would likely be a meltdown.

What would Liz-Beth and Sven have done? She had no idea. Before they died, Henry had eaten a wide variety of foods.

Heath reached across the table and laid his hand on top of hers. His touch was warm and reassuring. "Let me see what I can do," he murmured gently.

Before Claire could respond, he was off. Claire spotted him talking to the manager, then, to her amazement, he went out the front door of the restaurant.

The waiter returned with their drinks, and a basket of specialty breads.

Short minutes later, Heath came back in the front door, carrying a small paper bag. He handed it to the hostess and then rejoined them at their table. He winked at Claire. "Not to worry. We're all set."

He had just elevated himself to hero status. And that standing only went higher as the meal progressed.

He was patient with the kids. Attentive to Claire. Managed to keep the conversation going while they waited for the meal, and still color pictures with both children in turn.

When they had nearly finished their artwork, Heath told Henry, "That's a very good-looking fire truck, Henry. And, Heidi, that is a very nice mommy, daddy and baby that you colored."

"Are you a daddy?" Henry asked.

The waiter grinned as he set their plates in front of them.

Heath answered the query with the solemnity it was delivered. "No. I'm not."

"Why?" Heidi asked, eyeing Heath's steak, baked potato and steamed broccoli with a lot more interest than her own macaroni and cheese.

Henry wasted no time pushing his coloring aside and chowing down on the platter of peanut butter toast that had appeared before him. "Yeah, why?" he echoed, around a mouthful of food.

Claire touched a finger to her lips, gently reminding Henry to finish chewing before he talked.

"Hasn't happened yet," Heath said.

"Why?" Heidi pressed, as only an almost-four-year-old can.

"Because up until now I hadn't met the right woman." He paused and looked deep into Claire's eyes. And in that instant, she felt her entire universe shift.

"Funny," he said softly, "how quickly things can change."

Chapter Five

If the statement had come from anyone else, Claire would have declared it a line and a half. The look in Heath's eyes was sincere.

She knew how he felt.

Something was happening here.

Something quite unexpected…

"I have a baby," Heidi piped up, breaking the spell.

It was all Claire could do to hold in a sigh of regret.

Heath looked similarly disappointed. His glance told her he was fully prepared to pick up later where they had left off, at a time when Heidi wasn't waiting expectantly for a reply.

Heath turned his attention back to the children. "I know. Your baby doll's name is Sissy."

"But she couldn't come with us. She had to stay home. I can play with her later."

"I'm sure Sissy will like that." Heath cut some of his steak, fluffy baked potato and broccoli into preschool-size bites, under Heidi's watchful eye. He put it all on his bread-and-butter plate and slid it toward Heidi. She beamed in a mixture of gratitude and adoration, and tried a bite of his steak.

The waiter appeared with a tray containing two small

plates of French-fried potatoes and zucchini, and two little dipping dishes of ketchup. "I believe these are sufficiently cooled now, sir," he told Heath.

"Thank you." Heath put one dish between him and Henry, the other between Claire and Heidi. "I think we can all share these, don't you?" he said.

Henry eyed the fried veggies with a mixture of suspicion and longing. "I like peanut butter toast," he stated firmly.

"I can see. You're really chowing down on that. But if you decide you want something else, you can have some of this, too," Heath told him.

"That was very kind of you," Claire said, feeling her defenses melt a little more.

Henry picked up a fried zucchini stick and examined it on all sides before setting it down on the tablecloth beside his plate. He looked at Heath, curious again, just not about the food. "Do you have a dog?"

Heath seemed only slightly more surprised by the question, which had seemed to come out of nowhere, than Claire was. "No. I had one when I was a kid, though."

"So did I," Claire said. "Actually, we had several."

"I want a dog," Henry announced.

"When you're older, and can help take care of him, I promise you we will get you a dog," she agreed.

"What kind?" Heath asked, with a grin that was all male.

Claire had given it a lot of thought. "Golden retriever, I think. They're so gentle and patient with kids. But Labrador retrievers are great, too. Although they're more high energy than goldens."

Heath shrugged, the broad muscles of his shoulder straining against the fabric of his brushed cotton shirt. "It wouldn't be a problem if you had somebody to run with him. Or her."

Claire could imagine Heath racing over the ranch trails in the morning, a beautiful big dog at his side. She could imagine herself doing the same. She could even imagine them running together, the dog in the lead....

Her eyes locked with Heath's. Held. It was almost as if he knew what she was thinking, and wanted the same thing...

A discreet throat clearing disrupted the moment. Claire turned. Wiley Higgins was standing beside their table, hat in hand. "Saw you when I walked in." He inclined his head toward a ranching couple who had property a few miles from the Red Sage, obviously, his dining companions for the evening. "Thought I'd stop by and see if you had time to meet with me tomorrow afternoon. Say around four or five? Heath, I'd like you to be there, too."

Claire stiffened. "I think we've already said everything there is to say."

"I just want to throw some numbers at you. Discuss a few possibilities. I won't take much time, I promise," Wiley stated.

Claire turned to Heath. As usual when the discussion was on business, he was poker-faced and completely in favor of hearing Wiley out. Which meant, one way or another, she was going to have to listen to Wiley's latest proposal, too. If only to be able to explain to Heath why she didn't want to do it.

They settled on four o'clock the next day at the ranch office. Wiley said good-evening, and sauntered off. Claire sighed in frustration and turned back to Heath. "He doesn't give up, does he?"

Heath shrugged as if he had expected as much. "Wildcatters usually don't. That's what makes them so successful."

What about Heath? Claire wondered suddenly.

How far would he go to in the interest of business? Was this dinner all a part of his attempt to wear her down, when it came to making changes to the trust? Or was it, as she secretly hoped, part of a campaign to win his way into her heart? And possibly, her bed?

"ALL RIGHT, EVERYONE, it's time for baths and bed," Claire told the twins when they arrived back at the ranch.

"Can Mr. Fearsome read us stories with voices tonight?" Heidi asked.

"He does it better than you, Aunt Claire," Henry told her frankly. The tyke dropped his voice to a low growl. "When he talks, sometimes it's like this."

Heath grinned at the imitation and locked eyes with Claire. "I'm sure your aunt Claire reads a mean story," he said dryly, hoping she would ask him to stay.

"We like both ways," Heidi said. "Yours—" she pointed to Claire "—and yours." She pointed to Heath.

Claire looked at him, a question in her warm amber eyes.

"I don't mind," he said. He had nothing to go back to besides an empty cottage. Normally, he relished the quiet. Not now. Maybe, he thought, never again…

"Let me get them bathed and ready for bed, and then you can read to them."

Heath nodded. "Mind if I put on a pot of coffee?"

She continued gazing at him. "Mind making it decaf?"

"Sounds good."

The twins were so tired, one story sufficed. Claire kissed and hugged them each in turn. They nodded drowsily and lifted their arms to Heath.

Suddenly feeling more like a dad to them than a family

friend, he kissed them good-night, too. Then Claire and he walked back downstairs. "Coffee smells good," she remarked.

The fatigue of the day showed on her pretty face. Heath steered her in the direction of the living-room sofa. "I'll bring you a mug."

"You're going to spoil me," she warned over her shoulder.

He wished he could. Claire was the least spoilable woman he had ever met.

She was in a quiet, reflective mood when he returned.

He handed her her coffee and sat down beside her—not too close, but not too far away.

She had kicked off her boots and propped her sock-clad feet up on the coffee table strewn with adult magazines and children's storybooks. "Thanks for dinner tonight." She looked over at him shyly. "It was wonderful to get out like that."

He studied her feminine profile. "You don't go out much?"

A hint of sadness crept into her expression. "Not since Liz-Beth and Sven died." She blew at her steaming coffee and sipped. Perked up again. "Henry almost tasted a zucchini stick tonight."

Almost being the operative word. Puzzled, Heath asked, "Has he always been that picky?"

"Well. Yes and no. The first year or so he ate just about any food Liz-Beth put in front of him, where Heidi was a lot more cautious. She had to think about anything the least bit different before she put it in her mouth. Then they kind of reversed roles. And now Heidi wants whatever everyone else has. She's more interested in our dinners than her own, which you noticed. Thank you for letting her have some of yours, by the way."

"I'm glad she enjoyed it."

Lazily, Claire stretched her calves and wiggled her toes. "Plus, you saved the day by going over to the mercantile to get peanut butter and bread for Henry's toast."

Heath tore his eyes from the slender fit of her jeans. Like his, they were worn along the seams, faded, and soft as a glove. "The manager of the steak house was happy to accommodate us." He took off his boots and propped his sock-clad feet on the coffee table next to hers.

"Anyway, back to Henry's peanut butter obsession." Claire laid her head back against the sofa cushion. "It was the only thing that comforted him after the loss of his parents, so I wasn't going to take that away from him. The pediatrician said as long as the bread is whole grain and he gets milk every day, and a multivitamin tablet, he'll be fine. She expects him to outgrow it soon." Claire lifted the mug to her lips and took another sip. "The only thing he will eat aside from that is any kind of dessert." She grinned.

Heath returned her smile. "I noticed." After declining practically everything else at the restaurant, Henry had attacked his chocolate pudding and whipped cream with gusto.

"So I've been sneaking applesauce and pureed zucchini or carrots into cupcakes and cookies, every now and again," Claire said.

"Smart."

"And sometimes I can put a little fruit into a milkshake and get him to drink that, but it's pretty hit-and-miss. He really has to be in the mood. Although he does like apple and orange juice, so he gets some vitamins there."

Heath regarded her with respect. "Complicated."

She inclined her head. "I know he's just trying to exert what control he can over his universe. Heidi's doing the same thing. That's why she asks so many questions, and has this constant need to know what is going on." Claire paused. "It's almost as if she thinks if she works hard and long enough on the puzzle of why her parents passed on, that she'll be able to magically bring them back or something."

Heath had noticed what a little detective Heidi was. "How did they die?"

"They were driving home after a business trip. Bad weather hit unexpectedly. Their car went off the road and into a ravine. They were killed instantly."

"I'm sorry. That must have been very hard on you and the kids."

Claire nodded.

He took Claire's hand in his. She relaxed and twined her fingers with his. "Anyway, I know they're trying to make sense of their loss, as best they can, so…I try to be patient and understanding and make them feel as safe and secure as every kid should."

Sensing the children weren't the only ones in need of some tender loving care, Heath turned and pulled Claire into his arms. He tunneled his hands lovingly through her hair. Let his mouth fall to hers. At the first touch of their lips, she sighed and moved against him. With a low moan of satisfaction, he threaded his fingers through the curls at the nape of her neck and angled her head so their kiss could deepen. His other hand moved against her spine, urging her closer. Her mouth was pliant against his, warm and sexy. Her breasts were pressed against his chest. His tongue twined with hers. And still it wasn't enough.

Claire wasn't sure how it happened. All she knew was that one moment she was sitting next to Heath on the sofa, kissing, and the next she was on his lap, her bottom nestled against the hardness of his thighs, the proof of his desire pressed against the most intimate part of her. It didn't matter that they were both still fully dressed. Her insides tingled, and with that came the need to be so much closer.

She shifted again, wrapping her arms around his neck and straddling his lap. All the while, they kept on kissing. His hand worked its way under her sweater to the bare skin of her back, her ribs. Her nipples ached, until he reached up and covered her breasts with his palms. And Claire knew, even as she realized she had never felt this way before, that it was too much of a risk to continue.

She sighed, drew his hands away. "Heath…"

"I know." He kissed her again and again, each caress sweeter and slower and more loving than the last.

Finally, they broke it off altogether. "I better get going," he told her breathlessly, gazing into her eyes. "Otherwise…"

Otherwise, they'd be tempted to make love tonight.

And for so many reasons, Claire thought wistfully, that just couldn't happen.

"GOOD WORK ON THE Mitchelson trust," Orrin Webb told Heath at the bank the next morning.

"Thanks." He clicked the save icon on his computer and waited.

Orrin shut the door. Hands in his pockets, he strolled over to the window behind Heath's desk and gazed out at Main Street. Thanksgiving was ten days away, but the Summit, Texas, municipal workers were already hanging evergreen wreaths with big red velvet bows from every old-fashioned lamppost in the charming downtown area. The advent of the holidays made Heath more aware than ever of the lack of family in his life. It made him wish he had a wife like Claire and kids like the twins, and a home as warm and loving as the one they shared on the Red Sage Ranch.

He knew life wasn't perfect, but they made him feel like it could be. And that in turn made him want to trust his instincts again. Start actively looking for the woman who could give him the lasting love and commitment required to build a strong, enduring family—the kind that wouldn't be torn apart by different hopes and dreams...

Oblivious to the nature of Heath's thoughts, Orrin continued speaking about the business at hand. "The restructured trust is going to bring in a nice income from this point forward. The Mitchelson family won't be sorry they handed over the management of their inheritance to First Star Bank of Texas."

"That's good to hear," Heath said.

"Have you made any decisions regarding the trust for Claire Olander's niece and nephew?"

"I'm still considering what would be best." Hoping with ten more days she'd be able to pull off a miracle.

"What about the mineral rights on the land?"

"She and I have an appointment to talk with Wiley Higgins this afternoon. And there's another option, too." Briefly, Heath filled Orrin in on the latest regarding the Wagner Group.

Orrin paused. "You know, if you'd rather, I could assign this trust to Freddy Howitzer."

Freddy Howitzer was a numbers guy. Great with a certain kind of trust, where multiple beneficiaries were involved and the only thing that mattered at the end of the day was the amount of income generated from said trust. He was terrible when it came to situations that involved grief-stricken families. Freddy did not have the delicate people skills required—Heath did. "I can handle this," he told his boss. And he could do it in a way that would leave everyone happy.

Orrin moved closer. "Rumor has it you might be getting personally involved with the twins' aunt."

Guilt flared inside Heath. It wasn't like him to mix business and pleasure, but that was exactly what he was doing here. Reflexively, he pushed the emotion away and went back into business mode. There was no reason he couldn't handle this with keen, compassionate skill, same as any other trust. The fact it was going to be tricky to manage just meant he was going to have to be more on his toes.

As for the other...

"Since when did you start listening to gossip?" he chided his boss.

Orrin ignored Heath's attempt to sidestep the question. Looking more old-school than ever, he said, "You were seen having dinner with her and the kids last night."

Heath stood and moved restlessly to the window in turn. He looked across the street and saw a turkey poster on the window of Ruby's Barbecue, beneath a boldly lettered sign that said Preorder Your Smoked Turkey and Ham Now! Pick Up Thanksgiving Day!

Trying not to think what he'd be doing on Thanksgiving this year—fielding off invitations from pitying friends, or watching football and eating takeout alone—Heath turned. "Trust execs take clients to dinner all the time."

Orrin pushed his bifocals halfway down the bridge of his nose. "I didn't see an expense account for the meal."

That's because Heath hadn't filled one out. It hadn't felt

right to do so, since the dinner had been a lot more personal than professional in tone. Yet, beneath his desire to spend time with Claire and the kids, a legitimate purpose had been served.

Heath looked Orrin in the eye, able to be candid about this much. "I want Claire to trust me. To know that whatever has to happen to make the trust fiscally productive at the end of the day is the right thing. To do that, I have to get to know her and the kids. I have to win her confidence, since she owns all of the buildings and improvements on the ranch and is the children's legal guardian." He cleared his throat. "Ethically, you and I both know it's fine for me to be their friend, as well as their advisor, as long as I don't benefit financially from the relationship. Furthermore, in small communities like Summit, where everyone knows everyone else, this is the way it works. There are no strangers, unless someone is new in town."

"It's still a fine line," Orrin cautioned.

But one Heath would walk. Because it was the only way he could protect Claire and the kids. And whether they realized it or not, they needed his help.

"HAVE YOU HEARD ANYTHING from magazine and newspaper editors yet?" Mrs. Finglestein asked Monday afternoon, when she stopped in to the ranch office with her husband after another full day of bird-watching.

Heath came in right after them. He was early, but Claire had expected as much.

"No, I haven't," she answered.

"You'd think," Mr. Finglestein fretted, "given the size of those enormous gift baskets you sent with the DVDs, that someone would have at least called to say thank-you."

Ignoring the look of surprise—followed swiftly by

number-crunching disapproval—on Heath's face, Claire smiled. "The baskets were delivered just this morning. I doubt anyone's had a chance to even look at the footage of the ranch or the brochures we sent."

"Well, we're going to do everything we can to help you get your bookings up," Mrs. Finglestein vowed. "Because we are having a fabulous time."

"Thank you," Claire said.

"And we're going to try that Mexican restaurant you told us about this evening. So if you'd like us to bring anything back for you…?"

"I think we're good here. But don't forget to try the chiles rellenos. They're fabulous!"

"We certainly will!" Mr. Finglestein said.

When Wiley Higgins walked in, the mood in the room went from cheerful to tense in an instant. "Well…we'll let you get to…whatever," Mrs. Finglestein said. The couple departed gracefully.

Wiley shrugged out of the denim jacket he had on and opened his briefcase. "I imagine you want to cut straight to the chase." He handed over a folder containing a typewritten proposal for her to peruse. "I've talked to all the ranchers in the area and looked at the past specs for oil recovered from all the properties. The least amount pumped was from the Red Sage. Therefore, I'm figuring this property has the most oil still left in the ground.

"If you'll look at the numbers, given the price of crude right now, you'll see that if even one of the injection wells we're proposing to drill produces the on-average amount, you and your heirs will be sitting pretty for years to come. But I'm getting ahead of myself here. Before we go to contract on anything, we need more data. We need to send a vibrator truck onto the property, blast sound waves through the reservoir rock and measure the results on geophones."

He paused to take a breath. "We'll also need to move electric current through the rock to see if we can locate exactly where the oil-bearing strata are located. And then we're going to need to look at the rocks themselves, so we'll need to drill core samples from the likely locations, once we figure out where they are." His eyes lit up. "And best yet, we're going to pay you to allow us to further explore what your options might be. The fee schedule for all of this is on page ten of the handout I gave you."

Claire studied it. At first glance, the number was astounding, more profit than she would make in a year if the guest ranch was fully booked.

"You can see we're prepared to be very generous," Wiley said.

Claire could see why the Higginses sent Wiley out to make the pitch for their family-run operation. He was very persuasive, as well as enthusiastic.

"And all I have to do is let you drive one big truck—"

"Actually, it will be more like four or five large trucks, and half a dozen pickups, carrying the geologists and roughnecks," Wiley corrected.

"Onto my property. And then drill and shock and generally tear up the land, as well as all the hike and bike trails and xeriscape plants we've put in."

"I admit it will tear things up a bit. But think of the payback, if we hit oil."

"Actually," Claire said tightly, "I'm thinking of what this

little prospecting expedition would do to my guest-ranch business."

"Doesn't look like it's doing much, anyway." Wiley shrugged.

"Okay. That's it. You need to leave now." Claire grabbed his arm and his jacket.

"I understand this is a lot to consider." Wiley let her steer him as far as the porch outside the ranch office before digging in his heels. "And I can give you another week, tops, but I have to know before Thanksgiving. 'Cause otherwise we're going with our second choice ranch."

"Good luck with that," Claire said.

"Think about it," Wiley stated flatly. "Before you say no." He looked at Heath. "Talk some sense into her," he growled, then stalked off.

Claire turned back to Heath. As trustee in charge of the mineral rights on the Red Sage, he would make the final decision. Yet he had remained silent throughout the meeting. "Well? Don't you have anything to say?" she demanded.

Heath shrugged and looked her straight in the eye. "Would you listen if I did?"

Chapter Six

Claire looked at Heath intently. "I want to hear what you're thinking."

She had asked. It was only fair he enlighten her. Heath stood, legs braced, as if for battle. He pushed the edges of his suit coat back and propped his hands on his hips "You didn't even try to negotiate with Wiley."

Claire paced across the office. "What difference does it make what that man is willing to pay for the privilege of hunting for oil if I don't want him tearing up my property and chasing away all the wildlife?"

Although Heath had hoped to be gentle, he had no choice but to remind her of the facts. "The mineral rights belong to the kids. And the ranch is twenty-nine thousand acres."

Her chin took on the stubborn tilt he was beginning to know so well. "I'm aware of that." She jabbed the air with her index finger. "I'm also aware that you, as trustee, get to make the final decision about what is going to be done or not done in this regard."

"As I told you initially, I don't want to do anything that would not garner family support and approval, unless I absolutely have to."

"I hope you mean that."

"I do." Heath paused and looked her over. She was all fired up, more beautiful than ever. The soft denim fabric of her skirt hugged her hips and thighs, as nicely as a black V-necked sweater did her upper body. Opaque black leggings made the most of her spectacular legs. But it was the flush in her cheeks and the contentious pout on her lips that drew his glance again and again. "Unfortunately, time is running out," he told her reluctantly. "You've now got less than ten days to demonstrate the business is either showing a profit or soon to show a profit. And we both know that might not happen."

"I think it will," Claire argued.

"Why aren't you at least considering the possibility of letting Wiley Higgins wildcat for oil on the farthest reaches of the Red Sage?"

Claire went back to pacing. "First of all, the capped wells that Wiley is interested in aren't all that far from the ranch house, only two hundred acres or so south of here. Thanks to the efforts my father and mother put in, the property has grown into a very wild and beautiful nature preserve. It's where you run in the mornings, and I walk with the kids, and the Finglesteins go to bird-watch." Her voice hardened. "There's no way I'm letting them haul heavy equipment over the terrain, uncap those wells and send sound waves or electric charges into the rock. So negotiating for something I don't intend to do anyway would be pointless, as well as a headache I don't need right now. I'd rather the trust sell off part of the guest-ranch business first."

Heath nodded agreeably. "Okay. Now we're getting somewhere," he said.

CLAIRE DIDN'T WANT TO "get somewhere" if it meant giving up. She wanted to be a dreamer like her mom and dad had been. Only, she wanted to do what they hadn't been able to do. She wanted to be able to make her vision come to fruition in a way that was also profitable, instead of a tax liability that eventually drained every cent of oil money they'd inherited from her grandparents.

Heath sat on the edge of her desk and continued in a candid tone. "I talked to an executive with the Wagner Group this morning. They're expanding into the business retreat industry. And they're interested in at least taking a look at the Red Sage as a possible acquisition. The only problem is, they want full ownership and control of any property they acquire."

Claire suddenly felt as if the air had been sucked out of her lungs. "Which means I'd be out of a home and a job," she concluded.

Again, Heath shook his head. "Not necessarily." He paused to look into her eyes. "I explained your situation. They said they would be willing to consider you as property manager, as part of the deal, if they decided they wanted the ranch, and that's no sure thing."

"Look." Feeling trapped, she whirled, hands held out in front of her. "I can't stop you from selling the twins' half of the business, but there is *no way* I'm selling my half. So if you intend to look for buyers, even theoretically, you need to look for someone who is going to be okay with that."

Heath nodded. "Got it."

"Good." Claire breathed a sigh of relief. "So the Wagner Group is out."

Heath's expression remained impassive. "Got that, too," he noted dryly.

She searched his face. "You think I'm being overemotional about the oil thing, don't you?"

He shrugged.

Usually Claire didn't care what people thought, but it bugged her to have Heath believe she was behaving irrationally. Even if he was too polite to say so.

She grabbed her keys and strode toward the door. "Come over to the house with me. I want to show you something."

Heath rolled to his feet in one fluid motion. "Okay."

Claire locked up and they walked across the yard. The wind was whipping up, and the sky was cloudy. It was beginning to get dark.

"Where are the twins?" Heath asked as they entered through the back door.

It *was* unusual, Claire noted, having the ranch house this quiet as they closed in on the supper hour. She walked through the kitchen, snapping on lights. "Over at Mae Lefman's ranch. I asked her if she could watch them while I met with you and Wiley, but it had to be at her place since she's making pies to freeze for Thanksgiving Day." Claire hurried through the living room. "Have a seat while I—" The phone rang. She muttered under her breath and went back to get it. "Hello?"

"Claire?" Mae said.

In the background, Claire could hear the twins crying. She tensed in alarm. "What's going on?"

"They just noticed it was starting to get dark, and they got rather upset."

"Can you put them on speakerphone?"

"Sure."

"Kids?" Claire spoke into the receiver. "This is Aunt Claire."

"Where are you?" Heidi wailed.

"We want to go home!" Henry declared.

"I'll be right there," she said gently. "But stop crying, okay? Now I'm going to speak to Mrs. Lefman."

"Claire?"

"I'm driving right over." She hung up and turned to Heath. "I've got to go get the kids."

His dark-blue eyes mirrored her concern. "What happened?" he asked.

"I don't know." She grabbed her purse and keys. "Sometimes they get upset for no reason." She shrugged, wishing once again Liz-Beth and Sven were still alive, to be able to help with this. "It could be they're overtired."

Heath followed her toward the door. "Want me to go with you?"

She was about to tell him he didn't have to do that, then stopped. The truth was she could use some help. Because even when she got the twins home, she would have to prepare dinner for them. "If you wouldn't mind," she said, figuring what she wanted to show Heath could wait until later, "it would be great."

HEIDI BURST INTO TEARS the second she saw Claire walk into the Lefmans' cozy ranch house. Henry quickly followed suit.

"Where were you?" the little girl sobbed.

"We was worried!" Henry cried, then hiccupped.

"You could have gone to heaven!" Heidi declared, even more distraught.

Claire dropped her bag, knelt on the floor and stretched her arms wide. The twins ran into them, clinging to her with such heartfelt anguish that Claire felt her own eyes fill with tears. She held their small bodies close to her and pressed a kiss on top of each twin's head. "I didn't go to heaven," she said thickly. "I'm right here."

Mae, looking a little misty herself, pressed a hand to her heart. *"I'm so sorry,"* she mouthed to Claire. "I had no idea," she murmured. "I mean...they were fine. They were helping me with the pies, and then all of a sudden..."

Claire nodded and held the twins even closer. "You don't have to explain. It's happened a lot since..." *We lost Sven and Liz-Beth.*

Mae looked even more distraught.

With effort, Claire disengaged herself enough to get back to her feet. As she did, Henry caught sight of Heath, standing awkwardly in the doorway. "Mr. Fearsome!" he shouted jubilantly. Tears faded and he began to smile.

Heidi grinned, too. They raced to embrace Heath, both of them hanging on to his legs as if he were the answer to their prayers.

"Did you come to get us, too?" Heidi asked, lifting her arms to be picked up.

Heath effortlessly hoisted a forty-pound child in each arm. "I sure did," he said, looking as happy to see the twins as they were to see him.

"I'm hungry," Henry announced loudly.

"Me, too," his sister declared.

Mae chuckled, glad to see the children's good mood had been restored.

"Can we go to a restaurant with you again?" Heidi asked.

"We're going to have dinner at home," Claire interjected quickly.

Their faces fell.

"But Mr. McPherson is certainly welcome to join us," she concluded.

Heath looked at the upturned faces. "What do you think, guys? Should I?"

"Yes!" they shouted, their earlier fears forgotten.

"Then I guess we better get going," Claire said. "Heidi, Henry, say goodbye to Mrs. Lefman and thank her for watching you this afternoon."

They did as asked. Claire collected their jackets, expressed her own gratitude to Mae, and then the four of them headed out to her SUV.

"THERE'S SOMETHING I'd like to know." Claire looked at the twins as they finished up their dinner: peanut butter on whole wheat toast for Henry; turkey burgers, steamed broccoli and oven fries with ketchup for the rest of them. For dessert, fruit smoothies in front of everyone. "What kind of cake are you going to want for your birthday party?"

"Cupcakes!" Henry said.

"With sprinkles!" Heidi added.

Heath grinned, looking sexy and at ease in the ranch house kitchen, with the sleeves of his dress shirt rolled up to just beneath the elbow, tie off, the first two buttons on his shirt undone.

"I meant vanilla or chocolate or strawberry," Claire explained.

"Peach," Heidi declared.

That hadn't been one of the choices. But when Henry said, "Yeah, peach," Claire decided to go with it.

"Okay, peach cupcakes it is, with vanilla frosting and

sprinkles." This would be a good opportunity to sneak some fruit into Henry's diet.

"Finish up your smoothies, then we're headed upstairs for bed and bath."

They grinned. "Can Mr. Fearsome read us a story with voices?" Henry asked.

Trying not to think how much she was coming to depend on him, she assented. "Okay, but let's make it fast. Mr. Fearsome…I mean, Mr. McPherson…has had a long day. And I'm sure he's anxious to get back to his cottage."

But as it turned out, once the kids were tucked in, he looked anything but ready to depart. "You said you wanted to show me something earlier," he remarked, after they went back downstairs. "Before we got the SOS from Mae Lefman. What was it?"

Claire studied him. They'd had such a pleasant evening, she hated to bring business back into it. "You sure you're up for it?"

"Positive."

"Okay. Make yourself comfortable and I'll go and get it."

When she came down ten minutes later, Heath was in the kitchen, finishing up the dinner dishes. Gratitude filled her heart. "You didn't have to do this," she said.

He handed her a cup of coffee. "Not every night some-one makes me a turkey burger and a fruit smoothie, all in one meal."

"Liked it, huh?" *As much as I liked having you here with us?*

"The whole dinner was delicious. What do you have there?"

"Albums. My dad was bedridden for the last year or so of his life. It drove him crazy to be confined like that. To keep himself busy, he went through boxes of family photographs and compiled this history of the ranch. I thought you might be interested in looking at it. Hopefully it'll help you to understand what the Red Sage means to me."

HEATH SAT AT THE KITCHEN table, poring over the chronology that began back in the early 1900s when Claire's great-grandfather had purchased the Red Sage. "I hope you don't mind if I make the birthday cupcakes while you do that," she said.

Able to envision many more such evenings like this, Heath started to rise. "If you want me to help—"

"No. I've got it." She took a bag of peaches out of the freezer and put them in the microwave to defrost. "I'd much rather you look at that."

Heath settled in, content to read while Claire moved gracefully around the kitchen. "The ranch looks remarkably like it did back then," he noted. "Except, of course, the ranch house and barn were the only two buildings on the property."

Her lips quirked in a teasing half smile. "Just wait."

"So your great-grandfather raised sheep?"

"Yes." Claire put all the ingredients on the counter, next to the stand mixer. "He wasn't all that popular, since this was cattle country at the time."

"I gather there are problems trying to run two different types of animals so close together?"

Claire dumped sugar and butter in a bowl. "Especially when the land isn't fenced, and cattle had to be driven to the trains for transport to market."

"It looks like things changed when your grandfather Olander took over."

"Yes. He concentrated on breeding horses. But he never had the money or the patience to invest in really fine stock to start his herds, so he wasn't able to make much of a profit on the horses he did sell."

"It looks like the property went to seed a little."

Claire turned on the mixer. "It was definitely going downhill until they found oil. Then, as you can see by the condition of the house and how they expanded it, they were flush with money. To the point they didn't have to work, and they didn't."

Heath studied the photos of some of the drilling sites. The previously beautiful land had been ravaged. Ugly drilling platforms towered over dusty tracts, devoid of vegetation. Rough roads had been cut across the property and the oil workers had set up tent villages to sleep in. Later photos showed the land was populated with nodding donkeys as far as the eye could see. The area around every pump had been torn up, scraped bare and filled with deep ruts made by heavy equipment.

"This is what you're afraid will happen if you let Wiley Higgins uncap your wells and explore your property."

Claire spooned batter into paper cups, then slid them into the metal muffin tins. "It's hard to see how it wouldn't happen."

Heath turned the page. "Is this your father and mother?"

"Yes. They took over the Red Sage when my grandfather died. Their mission was to make sure all the wells—which were by then bone dry—were capped, all the extraneous equipment that had been left behind, hauled away. They brought in tractors and graded the land, to remove the deep ruts." She looked over at him. "Every year they brought in more native plants that didn't require a lot of water to flourish—like mountain sage, cedar and mesquite—and they spread wildflower seeds. They also limited the cattle ranching they did to a small portion of the property, where the stream runs through."

Heath flipped through more pages of pictures, as she slid the baking pans into the oven and set the timer. "It doesn't look like they ran more than fifty head of cattle at a time."

"It was almost a hobby for my father, since they still had oil money from the original boom. By the time my dad died, he'd run through all that, so my sister and I had a decision to make—sell the place, take the money and run...or find something else to do with it. Faced with losing it forever, we realized how much we loved it here, and we decided to do everything we could to keep the Red Sage in the family."

Heath finally understood why Claire was acting as she had. The Red Sage was the link not just to her heritage and her past, but to the family she had lost. "I'm glad you showed these to me," he said. He closed the last album cover, put it atop the stack he had perused, and stood.

"Liz-Beth and Sven wanted the twins to grow up here," she said quietly. "They wanted them to have the kind of carefree childhood we had, surrounded by the natural beauty of the land."

"It's more than that."

"You're right. I couldn't bear to leave here," she said thickly.

Heath took her in his arms. He held her close and smoothed her hair with the flat of his hand. "So you've never lived anywhere else?"

She leaned against him with a sigh. "I went to college

in Austin, and then lived in Dallas for five years after that—working as a marketing rep, and then a regional sales manager, for several different territories. I traveled all over Texas. As great as all the little towns and big cities were, nothing compared to the way I feel about this place."

"I'm beginning to see why," Heath murmured.

Then he did what he had been wanting to do all evening. He lowered his head and kissed her. And once they started kissing, they couldn't seem to stop. All the while, Heath knew it was dangerous to start anything that might shift the balance of a relationship that was so new and tenuous.

They had enough against them. But with her so near, and the need within him so strong, he found he couldn't walk away. Desire flowed through him in hot waves as she met the thrust and parry of his tongue with a steamy kiss. An ache started in his groin, spread outward. Unable to resist touching her, he ran his hands down her hips, over her back and shoulders, then down again, cupping the soft curve of her bottom, as he held her against him. Emotions ran riot inside him. He wanted her…now, even as the more rational part of him knew this was not the right time.

Claire felt she had been waiting forever to find happiness, to discover this incredible passion. Her knees were weak as he pinned her between the counter and his body, and she wreathed both arms around his neck, opened her mouth fully to the erotic pressure of his, let his tongue stroke hers. Needing more, she went up on tiptoe and arched against him.

So what if none of this was going to be simple or easy? Claire thought, completely swept up in her feelings as she savored the moment. Now that Heath understood her better, the two of them could get through this business phase, and then it would be easy to make the rest of it work. Heath cared about the kids. She could see it in his eyes. He might even be seriously interested in her—at least she hoped that was the case. Because she knew she was feeling something special for him.

Something way too wonderful to be interrupted by the oven timer going off....

But it *was* going off. Loudly. And the jarring noise brought them swiftly back to reality. To the fact that they were standing in her kitchen, with so much unresolved....

"Saved by the bell," Claire joked breathlessly.

Heath, too, seemed to think they needed to take things a bit slower. He exhaled, stepped back until they were no longer pressed together. "And the fact we still have a business to sort out. Once that's done—" with a tender look in his eyes, he let her go completely "—I'm going to pursue you with everything I've got."

Claire grinned, feeling happier than she had in a long time. "I'll look forward to it," she said.

Chapter Seven

Heath had just hung up the phone the next morning when Claire popped her head in the door of his office. "Got a minute?" she asked.

Surprised to see her at the bank, never mind looking so happy, he waved her in. "Can I get you a cup of coffee? Some orange juice?"

She shook her head and sank into the chair in front of his desk, setting her shoulder bag on the floor. "I can't stay. I just wanted to apprise you of the latest developments regarding the business." She tugged at the hem of her short brown skirt, which almost reached her knees. "Do you want the good news first or the bad?"

Heath tore his eyes from the lissome line of her calves. He liked the way Claire paired her skirts with similar-colored leggings. It was a sexy look, and one that suited her well. "The good."

Claire relaxed back in her chair. "Buzz Aberg, the travel editor from *Southwestern Living* magazine, called me this morning. He's taking me up on my invitation and coming to the Red Sage."

So she had pulled it off. Heath stepped around to the

front of his desk and sat on the edge, facing her. "That's great." He studied the mixed emotions on her face. "What's the bad news?"

Claire let out a beleaguered sigh, the motion lifting and lowering her breasts. "The only time Buzz has available between now and December first is Thanksgiving weekend, and he's already committed to hosting his entire extended family for the holiday. So I told him he could bring them all and we'd provide not only lodging but Thanksgiving dinner—on us."

Which would definitely not be good for the bottom line this month, Heath thought. Although exactly how far it would put her under would require another look at the books. "How many are in Buzz's family?" he asked calmly.

Claire wrinkled her nose and tugged at the collar of her turtleneck sweater. "That's the bad news. There are forty-six. Even doubling up, they are going need to nine of the cabins. Ginger is moving out tomorrow evening—her house is finally ready—but Wiley, Ms. Sturgeon and the Finglesteins plan to be there through Thanksgiving at least. So I was wondering if you would consider moving into the guest room in the ranch house a couple days before they're due to arrive, and bunk there until after the Aberg clan leaves."

Live under the same roof as Claire and the kids? See them last thing at night and first thing every morning? Heath didn't even have to think about it. "No problem. Be glad to help you out."

She raked her teeth across her lip. "But…? I see some hesitation on your face."

Not about being close to Claire and the twins; he was

certain that would be a good thing. He kept his eyes on hers. "It sounds like quite an undertaking."

She sighed and admitted, "It is going to be. For one thing, I've never cooked Thanksgiving dinner for everyone—that was always my sister's domain. She roasted the bird and planned the menu. I was just the sous-chef." Claire squared her shoulders. She met his eyes. "But I have all the recipes she used, as well as ones I have been collecting that look good. Not to mention that Ms. Sturgeon and the Finglesteins have agreed to help out with the cooking and serving in exchange for attending the meal…and another few days comp on their bill."

Heath frowned. "You understand this is going to bring your profits for the month down considerably."

"I also know you have to spend money to make money. *Southwestern Living* magazine has a circulation of 2.2 million. Plus, they run a Web site that gets over one hundred thousand hits per day, on average," Claire retorted stubbornly.

"If Buzz Aberg and his family have a great experience at the Red Sage, I'm hoping he will not only feature us in the magazine—probably the soonest that could happen is the spring—but that he will also list the ranch as a Must Visit on their Web site right away, along with a link to our own Web site. That kind of buzz—if you'll forgive the pun—could give us capital to expand almost overnight. So in my view it's worth the risk."

Her enthusiasm was contagious. "What can I do to help?" Heath asked.

"Spend every spare moment helping me get ready for the influx of visitors?" Claire murmured persuasively.

It would be a pleasure, he thought, particularly if it meant they wouldn't have to alter the business portion of the trust the following week. "Consider it done."

She stood and held out her hand, then changed her mind at the last minute and lightly kissed his cheek instead. She stepped back before the moment could turn intimate. "You really are a great guy."

Heath knew she thought so now. And would probably continue to think so if things worked out for the guest ranch the way she hoped.

If they didn't…if he had to be the bearer of bad news and sell the twins' portion of the ranch business to ensure the fiscal soundness of their trust…he doubted she would feel the same way. Which just meant he had to trust her marketing and sales expertise and redouble his efforts to help her. "So I'll see you this evening?"

"Plan on having dinner with us. And bring your math skills as well as your appetite. I'm going to need help figuring out how to adjust all the recipes to crowd size, so I can see what dishes are really doable, and which are not."

IT LOOKED AS IF A TORNADO had exploded in the play area of the ranch office, Heath thought several hours later. Books and toys were strewn everywhere. And the area surrounding Claire's desk was not much better. She had open cookbooks scattered all around her, taking up nearly every available inch of space as she sat cross-legged on the floor, making notes on a yellow legal pad.

Behind her, Heidi and Henry were equally busy. Henry had his tool belt and yellow hard hat on and was using his play wrench on every inch of the file cabinet. Beside him, Heidi had a child-size cleaning rag and toy bottle Heath assumed was meant to be spray cleaner, because she was pretending to pour some on the window ledge and then was rubbing the cloth over the pretend liquid.

"Looks like I got here just in time," he said, strolling in.

Claire looked up with a smile. The twins dropped what they were doing and raced to greet him.

"It's Mr. Fearsome!"

"Aunt Claire said you was going to come see us!"

Heath swung them up in his arms. Without thinking about it, he pressed a kiss on each curly head. "It's really good to see you guys," he said, as they hugged him fiercely.

"It's really good to see you!" they chimed almost in unison.

Claire unfolded her long legs and rose gracefully. She turned her face up to his. Heath realized he wanted to kiss her, too, but not in a casual greeting. He wanted to hold her and kiss her the way he had last night before they'd said goodbye, the way he couldn't kiss her at the bank this morning. In a manner that was definitely not G-rated. If the sudden glow in her cheeks was any indication, she was thinking the same thing.

Aware of their rapt audience, Heath contented himself with the thought that the greeting he would have given her, had they been alone, could come later. Much later. When they didn't have to worry about what anyone else thought.

"Hey," he said.

"Hey," she replied softly, looking into his eyes. "How was the rest of your day?"

"Good," Heath said as the e-mail signal on Claire's computer dinged.

"Hold that thought." She stepped around her desk and, still standing, punched in a few commands. As she read, the smile on her face faded. "Oh, no," she whispered.

"Problem?" he asked, setting first Heidi, then her brother on the floor.

Claire punched in another command on the keyboard, starting her printer. Seconds later, a page slid out of the high-speed machine. "Kids, would you mind if I spoke to Mr. McPherson outside for a moment?" she said.

They nodded and went back to their play area, while Claire ushered Heath out onto the porch, page in hand. The kids could see them through the glass, and vice versa. She watched them pick up their toys, then turned away so they couldn't see what she was saying. Although the sun was shining, the temperature was already dropping into the low fifties. She shivered in the cool breeze.

Heath took off his suit coat and draped it over her shoulders. "What's going on?"

"Big trouble." She leaned against the building, out of the wind. "The deluxe toy tool set I purchased for Henry's birthday present was back-ordered again. It should have been delivered today. Instead, it won't be here in time for his birthday party tomorrow afternoon."

Not good, Heath thought.

"It's the only thing he wants, and I've already gotten Heidi's heart's desire—a baby bath set. There's no time to order Henry's gift from any other Internet supplier, and the nearest toy superstore is in Fort Stockton."

Heath handed her his cell phone. "You want to call and see if they have it?"

Claire nodded, and rushed inside again to get the phone number. Through the glass, Heath could see that Henry was back to "fixing" things with his toy wrench, while Heidi was busy cleaning.

"Just another few minutes, kids," Claire said, and with a grateful look, she rejoined Heath, then made the call.

"Well, they have one tool set left, and they'll hold it for me, but only until close of business today, which is 8:00 p.m. So I'm going to have to go."

"I could run over for you," Heath offered. "I need to check on my townhome and pick up some more clothes and books, anyway."

"Thanks, but I think I better go myself, just in case it isn't in stock, despite what they said. If they *don't* have it, I'm going to have to pick out something else for Henry." She sighed wearily. "And if that happens, I'll have to pick something else for Heidi, too, because it wouldn't be fair for her to get the exact thing she asked for if Henry doesn't get the exact thing *he* wanted. I'll just save those items for Christmas presents."

"Parenting sure is complicated," Heath teased, impressed she took her duties so seriously. The twins had no idea how lucky they were.

Claire's voice cracked. "It's just…it's their first birthday without Liz-Beth and Sven, and I really want it to be as happy as I can make it for them."

Heath touched her shoulder gently. "I understand. Do you want me to stay here and babysit them? Or go with you?"

"I'd rather you go with me, if Mae can babysit."

As it turned out, Mae was only too happy to come right on over.

"Things are looking up again," Claire told Heath, handing him back his cell phone. Obviously relieved everything was going to work out after all, she stepped back inside the office, Heath following right behind.

WHEN CLAIRE LET OUT a gasp, Heath couldn't blame her for being distressed. The cover to her printer and fax machines had been pried off, while liquid hand soap was smeared across her entire desk.

"We're getting ready for company!" Heidi declared, as she pumped even more soap onto the edge of Claire's desk and rubbed it in with her cloth.

Henry shoved his toy wrench deep into the fax machine. "Yeah, and I'm fixing your machines!"

Claire rushed to stop the flow of any more gooey cleaner, while Heath went to rescue the toy wrench and snap the covers back on both fax and printer. Luckily, it appeared no real harm was done.

Claire got a roll of paper towels and some hot water and real furniture cleaner and put her desk to rights. "I appreciate all the help," she said kindly, then went on to explain in depth what was a toy and what was not.

Henry and Heidi listened intently.

What could have been a tearful crisis turned out to be a valuable learning experience.

"You were great with the kids," Heath told her, once they were on their way to Fort Stockton.

"Liz-Beth and Sven were great teachers. They always knew just what to say and do," she answered.

"Seems like that skill runs in the family."

A troubled look flashed in Claire's eyes, then disappeared. She shrugged off the incident. "It was my fault, anyway. I wasn't keeping a close eye on them."

Sensing she needed reassurance, Heath said, "They love you."

"I love them, too."

But it looked, Heath noted, as if Claire thought her love was not enough.

Silence fell. She opened up her briefcase and pulled out her yellow legal pad. Her mood much more subdued, she said, "As long as we have the time, would you mind giving me your opinion of these Thanksgiving dinner menus? Because I need to get this worked out this evening. I want several possibilities to present to Buzz Aberg tomorrow morning, for his family's approval."

By the time they reached the toy store in Fort Stockton, they had four different menus for him to choose from, as well as a list of decorations she was going to need.

Luckily, the deluxe tool kit was still on hold. Claire picked that up, as well as a few items for the goody bags the birthday party guests would be taking home with them. Heath picked up two presents, too, ones Claire was sure the twins were going to like.

From there, she and Heath drove to his place, a townhome in a new development geared for singles.

"Feel free to look around," he said when they walked in the door.

IT WAS AN INVITATION Claire couldn't ignore, particularly when seeing the way a man lived always told a woman so much about him. And she wanted to know who Heath was, deep down.

Switching on lights as he went, Heath crossed the beautifully appointed living room to a breakfast bar near the kitchen. Claire followed, drinking in every detail of the heavy, espresso-colored wood furniture and sleek cream sofa, silk draperies and eclectic accessories.

A display of sales brochures was prominently displayed

on the black marble countertop of the equally impressive, state-of-the-art kitchen. Next to it was a smattering of cards left by real-estate agents who had been there to either preview the property or take clients through.

"Well, it looks like I'm drawing some interest," Heath said.

"It's very nice," she commented, walking through to the formal dining room, which sported a beautiful table, buffet and Persian rug that all coordinated perfectly with the pale-green walls. "Like something out of a home décor catalog."

He flashed a puzzled smile. "Why do I think that's not so good, in your view?"

Because, she thought, it pointed out once again the disparity in their lives. A disparity she was no longer sure would be that easy to overcome. Not wanting to insult him for having great taste in furnishings and color schemes, she forced a smile and said, "This is great for a devoted bachelor like yourself."

He crossed the space between them in three easy strides. "I still hear a 'but' in there," he chided, taking her into his arms.

She warmed at the strength of those arms. "I can't really see me bringing Heidi or Henry here."

Heath threaded his fingers through her hair. "Why not?"

Claire's heart began to beat like a bass drum. "Because Heidi might smear liquid soap on all your beautiful furniture, while Henry's busy taking something apart that shouldn't be taken apart."

Heath brushed a strand of hair from her cheek and tucked it behind her ear. "You think that would bother me?"

Reminded how very much was at stake here, Claire said softly, "I think it would bother *me*."

"You know what I think?" He exhaled slowly and continued to study her in the quiet of his townhome. "I think you're making excuses."

Claire glanced away. "Excuses about what?"

"About why you and I aren't going to work."

She gulped. That was exactly what she'd been thinking. She moved past him and, because there was no place else to go downstairs, headed up the staircase. She shot him a quelling look over her shoulder. "I think we can be friends."

He looked as if he wanted to shake her or kiss her senseless—she couldn't tell which. "Suppose I don't want to be just friends."

Claire paused at the top of the stairs and watched as he climbed to her side. "Then what do you want?" she demanded.

"Truthfully?" He stared at her, a wealth of feeling in his eyes. "This."

He backed her up against the wall and caged her with his body. She could feel the heavy thudding of his heart and see the sensuality in his smile as his head lowered slowly, to hers. She didn't want to give in to him, into something that seemed stronger than the both of them, but his will was fiercer than hers. With a low moan, she tipped her head back to give him access. Their lips meshed, and the world fell away. All she knew, all she wanted to know, was the comfort of his mouth moving over hers, and the magical power he seemed to hold over her heart. As she savored the taste of him, she couldn't remember anything ever feeling this right, this real, this solid.

"Tell me you want this, too," Heath said, between sweet, seductive kisses.

"I want this, too," she whispered, winding her arms

around his neck and pressing her breasts against his chest. Another shiver of excitement went through her. "So much."

Then his mouth was on hers again in a kiss that was shattering in its possessiveness. He deepened the pressure, his palms on her back drawing her intimately near. He kissed her as if he was in love with her and would be for all time. As if he meant to have her. Hearts pounding, they kissed their way down the hall, into his bedroom. Wrapped in each other's arms, they tumbled onto his king-size bed. As they settled onto the pillows, the affection in Heath's eyes was all the incentive she needed. She could hardly believe this was happening, and yet there was no denying the need, the yearning, deep inside her.

Driven to abandon, she surrendered to the feel of his hands slipping beneath her clothing to touch her breasts, her tummy, her thighs. Her clothes came off, with his help. His came off with hers. Naked, they slid between the sheets, with nothing between them but desire. Aware she had never felt sexier in her life, she kissed him passionately, savoring every second of their coming together.

When the kiss ended, he made his way slowly down her body, exploring every curve and dip with almost unbearable tenderness. Urgency swept through her as he suckled one breast, then the other, before shifting lower still, to her navel, her abdomen. Claire trembled as he reached between her legs and found the sweet spot there. She shifted restlessly, only to have him hold fast, and then his mouth was on her in the most intimate of kisses. Longing streamed through her and she came apart in his hands.

And then it was her turn to please him, bestowing on him the same languid exploration of his hard, strong body, until it was more than he could take.

He shifted so she was beneath him once again. Sliding a hand beneath her hips, he lifted her and surged into her with one smooth stroke. She gasped at the mesmerizing feel of him, buried deep inside her, and then all was lost in the power of their joining. She wanted him, wanted this sweet, magical pleasure....

His bedroom grew hot and close, their bodies slick and warm. Together, blood running hot and quick, they moved toward the height of ecstasy, losing all in the shattering pleasure.

HEATH ROLLED ONTO his side, taking Claire with him. Lying face-to-face, they both worked to slow their breathing. Neither could seem to stop grinning. And he had a feeling he knew why. He had never felt a greater contentment.

"Wow," Claire exclaimed tremulously at last.

"Wow," Heath echoed.

They smiled at each other some more.

Then, as Heath feared, the moment began to feel awkward. Sensing Claire was feeling some remorse—for how quickly and unexpectedly they had ended up in bed together tonight—he stroked a hand down her back. He knew she didn't do things like this casually, any more than he did.

Sex came with strings, and with those strings, commitment.

"If only I could stay here forever," she murmured, conflict evident in her amber eyes. Extricating herself from his arms, she sighed in regret. "But I can't. I've got a babysitter to get home to."

He watched as she rolled away from him and, clutching the sheet to her bare breasts, sat up on the edge of his bed. Her blond curls all tousled, cheeks flushed, lips swollen from their kisses, she made a delectable sight. She looked so beautiful he wanted nothing more than to make love to her again and again.

But it wasn't going to be.

Not tonight.

His eyes still on her, Heath stood reluctantly and began to dress. She needed time to process this. He could see that. He would give it to her, even though restraining his own urges and staying away from her right now was the last thing he wanted. "This is just the beginning, Claire," he told her softly.

"Sure you know what you're signing on for?" she teased, dressing in turn. The only thing that gave away her discomfort was the slight trembling of her fingers, and the fact she couldn't quite manage the zipper on her skirt, not without his help, anyway. "Because I'm a package deal now, and the twins are quite a handful."

Letting her know with a look and a touch they had nothing to be ashamed about, Heath said gruffly, "That's nothing I can't manage." And to prove it, he took her into his arms and kissed her soundly once again.

And he kept kissing her, until there was no more denying it—the physical passion between them was a force too powerful to be denied. Alone, it might not be a sufficient foundation for a relationship, but it was a good start. A helluva good start. For now, Heath would be content with that.

Chapter Eight

Claire had just finished setting out the breakfast buffet when Heath walked into the ranch house dining room. He looked incredibly sexy and approachable in a charcoal suit, light-green shirt and striped tie. As their eyes met, the memories of the night before came back in a rush. Claire flushed. Heath smiled with an optimism in his eyes that mirrored her own.

Maybe this was going to work out after all, she thought. Certainly, she could imagine herself with Heath, meeting like this every morning for weeks and months to come...and not just because he was renting one of her cottages.

The twins bolted toward him. "Are you coming to our birthday party today, Mr. Fearsome?" Henry asked.

Heath hunkered down so he was on eye level with the dynamic duo. "What time is it?"

Heidi and Henry both wrapped their arms around his broad shoulders and tilted their faces up at him, while Claire supplied the details. "Twelve-thirty to one-thirty—at the picnic pavilion in the park."

"All our friends from preschool are going to be there!" Heidi announced.

"Lunch is provided," Claire added.

"And cupcakes! With candles!" Henry declared.

"I would be delighted to come to your party," Heath told them, and the twins hugged him happily.

"Let's let Mr. McPherson have his breakfast," Claire said, disengaging them gently.

The children ran off to go play, talking excitedly amongst themselves. "You're looking pretty this morning," Heath said, once they were alone.

She felt pretty—from the inside out. Claire handed him a plate from the buffet. "Careful, or everyone who sees us is going to know…"

"That the two of you are falling in love?" Mrs. Finglestein finished, strolling into the dining room. She and her husband were clad in their usual khaki outfits. "Dears, that is old news."

Mr. Finglestein nodded toward his wife proudly. "Can't hide anything from her. She's got a sixth sense about these things."

"You two are going to make it for the long haul," she predicted.

Ginger strolled in, every bit the real-estate professional. Bypassing the sumptuous buffet, she headed straight for the coffee. Clearly not all that happy about the news that Claire and Heath were hooking up, she poured herself a cup and stirred in artificial sweetener. "Whatever the case…if you decide to buy sooner rather than later, Heath—or if you decide to sell the ranch after all, Claire—I've got listings I can show you both."

"Thanks," Claire said, preparing a breakfast tray to take down to T. S. Sturgeon's cottage. "I'm not selling."

"Good," the Finglesteins said in unison.

Ginger glanced at Claire with an enigmatic look on her

face. Then she turned to Heath. "I'm moving out this evening, and I could use a little help loading things into my car. Will you be around?"

"Be my pleasure to assist you," he replied, ever the Texas gentleman.

Wiley Higgins strode in. He helped himself to two of the breakfast sandwiches and a bowl of fruit.

"How's the search for oil going?" Mr. Finglestein asked him.

"I'm close to a deal with a rancher down the road," the wildcatter said, pouring coffee into his thermos.

"I hope you're able to close it," Claire said sincerely.

Wiley shrugged. "It's not my first choice," he said, giving her a look that let her know she still had time to change her mind.

A horn sounded in the front driveway.

Startled, Claire looked out the window. The driver from the car pool was early. Glad for any excuse to cut off further talk about mineral rights and oil exploration, she rushed out into the hall. "Heidi! Henry! Grab your backpacks. It's time to go!"

"CLAIRE DOESN'T KNOW the VP from the Wagner Group is in town, does she?" Ginger remarked as she and Heath walked out to their respective cars, for the morning commute to Summit.

"How'd you hear about that?" Heath asked, feeling a little guilty that he hadn't told Claire yet. He'd meant to but the time had just never seemed right. And to be truthful, he wasn't sure how she would take the news.

The real-estate agent shrugged. "As the top-producing broker in the area, I tend to get wind of everything happening or about to happen in the business community. And I had dinner with Ted Bauer last night. He wanted my opinion on the area in general, and the Red Sage in particular, and I gave it to him."

"I hope it was a positive review."

Ginger grew reflective. "I told him the ranch has the potential to become a great spa if a company like the Wagner Group were to buy it and run it."

Heath looked at the mountains in the distance and thought once again how beautiful it was out here. He turned back to Ginger. "Claire's not looking to sell out completely."

"In my view, that's the only way it would work, if you want to turn this place into a real moneymaker. Face it, Heath. Consumers want luxury these days. Not down-home ambience."

Depends on the consumer, Heath mused silently. He got his car keys out of his pocket. "Do me a favor and don't mention this to Claire."

"Don't worry. I'm not going to do anything to get on Ted Bauer's bad side. If the Wagner Group does come to the area, their employees are going to need homes. I plan to be first in line to sell to them."

And no doubt would succeed, Heath realized, as he said goodbye to her and got in his car.

He respected Ginger's ambition. Her tendency to mow down anyone in her path, professionally or personally, was less admirable.

He favored a more tempered approach.

He wanted to be known as a stellar businessman—with heart. That was not an easy line to walk.

Particularly when he was becoming as involved as he was with Claire and the twins.

Romancing her would not be uncomplicated, given all the

commitments she juggled. Nevertheless, Heath was certain he was up to the challenge.

Dealing with the business of trying to ensure the twins' trust was fiscally productive was a different matter entirely. He understood Claire nixing any further oil exploration on the Red Sage. However, she still had to make changes that would put the ranch—and hence the twins' half of the trust—on firm financial ground.

Heath hoped that she would listen with an open mind to what he and Ted Bauer planned to propose to her this afternoon. In the meantime, he had work to do, two presents to wrap and a birthday celebration to attend.

Normally not all that much of a party person, Heath found himself watching the clock all morning. Unfortunately, just as he was heading out the door, he got a call from an important client he had been trying to reach for several weeks.

By the time their business was concluded, the twins' party had already been under way for at least fifteen minutes.

Heath hurried to his car and drove to the park. He could see the balloons bobbing from the posts of the picnic pavilion as he hurried to wrap the presents with the paper and Scotch tape he had purchased on the way into work.

Finished, he strode quickly across the grass. It was clear from the disarray of paper plates and cups that the kids had already finished their meal of pizza. Claire was standing in a group of casually attired mothers who were supervising the dozen or so four-year-olds in what looked like a finger-painting activity.

"You see," Claire was saying, "if you dip your hand in the paint and spread your fingers out to one side, your thumb the other and then press down, it looks like you've made a Thanksgiving turkey! You can do one in every color. All you have to do is wipe your hands on the paper towel and... Heath!"

"Mr. Fearsome!" The twins leaped up in unison and ran to greet him. Dodging the two badly wrapped presents in his hands, they barreled into him and hugged him fiercely, one on each side, their tiny hands pressing into the back of his coat jacket and the front of his thighs.

Claire gasped.

A collective groan swept through the group of mothers in attendance.

"You came to our party!" Henry said. "You're here!"

"And slightly more colorful for the effort," Claire observed dryly. "I am so sorry," she said, offering a look of sincere apology.

"It's okay," Heath said, trying not to calculate what the suit had cost.

"It's washable finger paint, which probably means it should come out of a dry-cleanable fabric."

"I'm sure it will." Even if it didn't, it was worth it to Heath, given the hero's welcome he had just received. He'd never had kids look at him as adoringly as the twins did, never been as emotionally attached to any two children as he was to them.

Claire admonished the children to thank Heath for the presents, which they did, then shooed the kids back to the finger-painting table. They resumed working on their colorful collage of Thanksgiving turkeys, while Claire returned with a roll of paper towels. "Might as well blot off what we can," she said.

To make things easier, Heath took off his suit jacket. Claire dabbed that while he did the front of his trousers.

"We saved you some pizza," Claire said.

"Yeah." Henry came back to report. "I ate pizza, too, but I saved my peanut butter sandwich for later. You can have some. I'll share it with you if you want."

Knowing how seriously Henry took his preferred rations, Heath patted the little boy's shoulder. "Well, thanks, Henry." Heath briefly caught Claire's eye. They exchanged looks of shared wonder. "I'm glad you had some pizza," Heath continued.

"Yeah," Henry admitted, as if somewhat surprised. "It was good!" He raced off to be with the other kids.

"Wow." Heath turned to Claire.

"I know," she murmured. She handed him a plate of food and a glass of iced tea. "That was a big step for the little guy."

For them all, Heath thought. It meant Henry was finally settling in.

Noting Claire looked as happy as the twins about his attendance, Heath ate quickly, then eager to be even more involved, helped with the last of the finger painting.

Next came the musical portion of the party—a rousing rendition of the Chicken Dance, complete with a lot of bobbing and arm flapping and *bwack bwack bwack bwack bwacks*. And then the Hokey Pokey. Although he had never been particularly fond of either activity, Heath somehow found himself out on the grass, in the middle of the group. The other mothers danced, too—he wasn't the only adult out there—but he was pretty sure that of all of them, he looked the most foolish, a fact confirmed by the amused grins of the other adults in attendance.

The twins took turns batting their birthday piñata, until all the candy came tumbling out. Finally, it was time for the peach cupcakes with vanilla frosting and sprinkles.

"Do we get to make a wish?" Heidi asked Claire.

"And it has to be a secret, right?" Henry added.

"Yes, you get to make a wish before you blow out the candles. And the wish is supposed to be a secret."

"'Cause otherwise," one of the other children called out, "the wish won't come true."

"Yeah, if you don't tell anybody what it is, it will come true!" another child explained.

That wasn't a promise Heath would have made, given the unpredictability of children's whims and the probability of any desire coming true. Suppose, for instance, Henry wished for a pet elephant in the backyard. Obviously, that would not come true.

But then, maybe if that were his wish, Henry wouldn't expect it to come true. These were pretty bright kids, after all....

Claire finished lighting the candles, four for each twin. She took a few pictures then led the children and adults in song. With closed eyes, Henry and Heidi held hands and made their secret wishes.

"Okay. Open your eyes and blow out the candles!" Claire said.

They blew as hard as they could, while everyone clapped and cheered, and finally, the flames went out. The twins beamed with pleasure. Heath was happy to note that Claire's fear that this first birthday without their parents would be traumatic for them hadn't been realized.

He hung around while Claire handed out gift bags to every child who'd attended. Along with the twins, he helped her carry the coolers, and leftover cupcakes, and presents to her SUV.

"Thanks for coming," she said, almost shyly, "and being such a good sport. And not to worry, I'll handle your dry-cleaning bill."

Heath glanced down at his suit trousers. "It's okay. It'll give my colleagues at the bank something to rib me about. Meantime, are you free later this afternoon—say, around four o'clock?"

"Yes." She tensed a little. "Why?"

Heath wished he didn't have to force this on her, but his job required that he do so. "Ted Bauer, a VP from the Wagner Group, is in town. He and I are going to talk, and I'd like you to be part of the conversation. To make it easier for you, we can come to the ranch office."

Some of the happiness left Claire's eyes. "You know how I feel…"

Yes, Heath did, but he would not be protecting the twins' financial interests the way he should unless he followed through on this. "It's important you consider all the options, just as I intend to do."

Claire looked as if she wanted to argue, then put on her businesswoman's hat and reconsidered. "I'll see you in a few hours then."

CLOUDS ROLLED IN FROM the north as the afternoon progressed. The poor visibility and slick roads made driving hazardous and it was pouring rain by the time Heath got to the ranch. Ted Bauer was already opposite Claire by the time he walked into the ranch office. The short, affable man with thinning red hair was exchanging pleasantries with her, while the twins were once again making a wreck of their play corner, seeming unusually hyper.

"Sorry I wasn't here to do the introductions," Heath apologized cheerfully, shaking the rain off his finger-paint-stained business suit.

"No problem. Claire and I were just getting acquainted," Ted said.

"The Wagner Group runs a much more high-end operation than I do," Claire told Heath.

"Which on the surface is no problem," Ted stated, "should we eventually be interested in acquiring the Red Sage Guest Ranch and Retreat as one of our properties. We could always use the current cottages to house staff."

It was all Claire could do not to wince, Heath noted.

"The cottages are nice," Heath found himself saying. "I'm living in one right now."

"Nice meaning rustic," Ted corrected, his attitude as polite as it was candid. "Our properties cater to the superrich. Their expectations include only the very best. Thousand-thread-count linens, twenty-four-hour room service, on-site massages, nutritional consultations, trainers, even diagnostic blood tests and bone scans."

Claire blinked in amazement.

Ted continued, "Some of our competitors are taking it a step further by offering clairvoyants, astrologers, sex therapists and tarot-card readers, but we're not prepared to go that far."

She sighed and shook her head. "I can't see Red Sage ever being part of that…"

"No, of course not," Ted assured her quickly. "But if we came in, we'd bring it up to par."

Claire shot a look at Heath, then another at Ted. "I think there's been some miscommunication. I'm not looking to sell out completely. In fact, I won't even consider it."

Ted frowned impatiently. "That's the only way the Wag ner Group will do business. Apparently you two have som matters to iron out, and our negotiations can't continue unt you do so." Putting an abrupt end to the meeting, he left h card, told Claire to call him if she changed her position, an strode out into the rain.

Heath turned back to Claire. "This meeting today was ju a starting point in negotiations," he said, unable to contai his frustration with her inflexible attitude and the quick diminishing timeline he had to come up with a solution. "(at least it should have been," he amended more gently, "ha you not shot down any further talks right out of the gate."

CLAIRE LOOKED AT HEATH, her mouth dry. She knew th tone. Her skeptical friends had used it when she'd told the she planned to return to the ranch and convert it to a gue lodging and retreat facility. It was the tone that said she w a naive fool, best protected from her own fanciful dreams success. It was the voice of someone who felt he knew bet than she did, what was right for her and the Red Sage.

She'd thought Heath supported her in her quest to ma her vision a success. Had she been wrong? With difficul she forced herself to ask, "Are you saying you think I shou sell out completely?"

"I'm saying that partial interest in a real moneymake a lot better than full interest in a business that's perpetua in dire straits. Fortunately, Ted is enough of a professio to be open to further discussion if contacted."

"Meaning what, you're going to override my feelir on this?"

"Technically…"

"I know you can do it, Heath. I'm asking if you're going to betray me."

He was silent. Which was, Claire thought, all the answer she needed. "I see." She took him by the elbow and pushed him toward the door. "Thanks for stopping by."

He held out his hands in supplication. "Claire. We need to talk about this."

"Not now."

"When then? Time is running out."

As if she didn't know that! "When I get my thoughts together, I'll let you know." She propelled him through the portal and shut the door behind him.

"Are you sad, Aunt Claire?" Heidi asked.

"I think she's mad," Henry decided.

"It's just business," Claire assured them with a brisk, motherly smile.

"Business isn't fun," Henry said.

"But birthday parties are," Heidi stated. "Can we have another birthday party tomorrow?"

Glad for the respite from her dark thoughts, Claire knelt to help them pick up their toys, "No, kiddos, we can't. Birthdays only come once a year."

A fact she was very glad of, two and a half hours later, when she finally readied the twins for sleep, read them a story and tucked them in bed. They had completely exhausted her, and she still had so much to do to get ready for Buzz Aberg and his guests.

With a sigh, she went down to the dining room, where she had set up a crafts area. She had just finished the first horn of plenty when a knock sounded on the front door and she went to answer it.

Claire found the rain letting up, but braced herself against the cold gusty wind that blew through the yard. Heath stood on the other side of the portal with a resolute look on his handsome face.

She'd seen him helping Ginger load her things in her car earlier. He'd still been in his suit and had gotten pretty wet. He looked as if he had shaved and cleaned up since—he was now clad in a black windbreaker, jeans and scuffed Western boots.

Trying not to shiver in the chilly blast, she folded her arms in front of her and lifted her chin. "I'm not ready to talk to you just yet."

"That's okay." He flashed a cynical half smile. "I don't mind doing all the talking." He breezed on in.

She sighed and let him pass, shut the heavy oak door behind him, then went to the thermostat in the hallway to switch on the heat. "I mean it, Heath. I haven't had time to collect my thoughts."

He slipped off his jacket and hung it on the coat tree next to the stairs. Taking her hand, he walked with her into the living room, where he guided her to the end of the sofa, choosing a wing chair himself, so they were face-to-face. "Then perhaps you could listen," he said in a soft, serious voice. "I conceded to your wishes, even though, technically, I didn't have to take them into consideration. I didn't give Wiley permission to explore for oil on the land the twins inherited, without your consent."

Claire swallowed. "And I appreciate that," she said even though her temper was rising once again. "What I didn't appreciate was the suggestion that I should sell out to the Wagner Group!"

"Even if it meant you wouldn't have to worry about finances for the rest of your life, and neither would the twins? Even if it meant you could possibly work a deal to have a job as property manager—and the executive pay that goes with such responsibility? To have the ranch house and perhaps several of the cottages for your own use?" He ran a hand through his hair. "Did you think of any of those options? Did you consider that, with the right advocates negotiating on both sides, you could end up with an arrangement everyone will be happy with?"

With it put that way, she did feel like a fool.... Claire sighed. "Look, I know from a strictly numbers perspective it makes sense."

"But...?"

"But it feels like if I do this I'd be taking the easy way out—and giving up on the dream I shared with Liz-Beth and Sven. And that," she concluded, "feels like a betrayal."

Chapter Nine

"Liz-Beth and Sven would understand it's too much for one person to take on," Heath told her. The fault here lay in the way the trust had been set up, in the fact that Liz-Beth and Sven had died before the business could get up and going. He knew Claire had done the best she could, under very trying circumstances. But there was no shame in reevaluating and going in a different direction than originally expected. Businesses did it all the time.

He paused to look deep into her eyes. "You have something more important to consider," he murmured. "You have the twins and their financial futures, their parents' wish that they grow up on the Red Sage—even if it is in a slightly different way than their parents envisioned. You have to protect that first, and worry about any career goals and aspirations you and your sister and her husband had, second."

Claire was studying him soberly when a small voice piped up from the bottom of the staircase.

"Aunt Claire?" Henry called plaintively. "I waked up."

"I waked up, too," Heidi said.

Heath turned in time to see the children trudge unhappily

across the room. Both were rubbing their eyes and appeared to have been crying.

He felt an unexpected lump in his own throat.

"Hi, Mr. Fearsome," Henry said, bypassing Claire's arms to climb onto Heath's lap.

Looking just as unhappy, Heidi slid onto Claire's. "Yeah. Hi, Mr. Fearsome," she said sleepily.

Claire wrapped her arms around her niece.

Deciding that was a good idea, Heath did the same with Henry.

"What are you two doing awake?" Claire asked, looking sweetly maternal as she hugged the little girl close. "Did you have a bad dream?"

They locked glances for a second, seeming to communicate the way many twins did. Finally, Henry exhaled slowly and said, "We're sad."

A flicker of pain flashed in Claire's eyes. Heath felt an answering pang in his gut.

She prodded gently, "Can you tell me why you're sad?"

Even though, Heath guessed, she probably already knew. It was hard to lose a parent. Even harder to lose both when you were that young.

Another silence fell.

Heidi rubbed the soft fabric of her flannel pajama top between her fingers.

Henry rested his head on Heath's shoulder, giving Heath a taste of what it would feel like to be a dad, rather than just a friend of the family. And not just any dad, but Henry and Heidi's…. And "Aunt Claire's" husband.

Finally, Heidi murmured, "Because we miss Mommy and Daddy."

"Do you think they're sad, too?" Henry asked, looking at Claire, and then up at Heath.

"Because they didn't get to come to our birthday party today?" Heidi added.

Realizing how bittersweet today must have been for the kids, Heath felt a pressure behind his eyes. And that was weird. He never cried....

Claire held out one arm to Henry. He slid off Heath's lap and into her embrace. Holding both twins close, she lovingly stroked their curls and said, "Actually, your mommy and daddy kind of were there with you today."

"But we didn't see them!" Henry protested.

Obvious frustration at being unable to communicate with the kids as well as she wanted to showed in Claire's amber eyes. "I meant in spirit," she corrected softly. "They were watching over you from heaven."

The twins regarded her uncomprehendingly.

Claire tried again. "I know it's confusing, because we can't see or hear Mommy and Daddy. But they can see and hear us, and they're watching over us and keeping us safe all the time." Claire stroked her palms down the little ones' backs in a comforting massage. She bent her head and pressed a kiss to the top of each child's head. "If you shut your eyes and think real hard you can feel their love. When you do that, it wraps around you like a big warm blanket."

The twins smiled faintly at the analogy.

While Heath gazed on admiringly, Claire paused and looked into the eyes of each. "And you know you don't ever have to worry, because you've got all the love they ever gave you right here in your hearts." She touched the center of her chest. "And the love you felt for them is there, too. It will always be there, deep inside you, making you feel good." Her voice thickened, her own emotions welling as she continued, "So let's try it, okay? Let's all close our eyes and remember what it was like to feel Mommy's and Daddy's arms around us, holding us close, holding us safe."

In unison, everyone's lashes fell, shuttering their eyes. Slowly, Heath saw their breathing even out, their small bodies relax in their aunt's loving embrace. "Can you feel it now?" Claire murmured.

Heath could. He'd never felt more love in his entire life. Hadn't even know, until now, it was possible.

Both children nodded. "Good," she said. "So," she added after another long, soothing cuddle, "are you ready to go back to bed now?"

Both children opened their eyes. Sadness faded. Contemplation appeared.

"Can we put cupcakes on a plate first?" Henry asked.

Claire appeared as surprised by the unexpected request as Heath felt.

"With milk. Like we do for Santa Claus, with cookies," Heidi explained.

"So Mommy and Daddy can have birthday cupcakes, too, when they come to watch over us tonight, while we sleep," Henry said.

Clearly, Heath noted, this was something the twins had discussed.

Her surprise fading as quickly as it had appeared, Claire nodded. "I think that's a wonderful idea!"

Heath and the twins went with her to the kitchen. They got out two plates, two cupcakes, two napkins and two glasses of milk. "Let's put them by the fireplace," Henry said.

"Yeah, where we put the cookies for Santa," Heidi explained.

Once that was accomplished, Claire had the children say good-night to Heath.

Before she could herd them up to bed, Henry turned to him and said, "I want Mr. Fearsome to tuck us in, too!"

"SORRY ABOUT ALL THAT," Claire said after they finally returned downstairs.

"You handled their grief really well," Heath remarked.

"Thanks." She let out a sober breath, then raked both hands through her hair, looking a little frazzled. "It's hard to know what to do or say sometimes. I mean, I've had expert advice. But there's nothing that can prepare you for the queries that come up in the moment."

"It's not just the twins. You miss Liz-Beth and Sven desperately, too, don't you?"

Moisture glittered in her eyes and was promptly blinked back. She wandered into the dining room, stood staring down at the crafts material scattered across the table. "As difficult as the twins' birthday was, I know Thanksgiving and Christmas are going to be even harder. Especially Christmas," she said hoarsely.

Heath had seen firsthand how strong she was in all aspects of her life. And how tenderhearted and compassionate, too. But it was her determination to be there for the twins whenever they needed her that would continue to carry her through the tough times. "You'll manage," he told her, meaning it.

Without warning, the tears she'd been holding back spilled over her lashes. She pressed a hand to her lips and stifled a small, anguished sob. Heath didn't have to think about what to do next; he put his arms around her and pulled her close. She melted against him, her body trembling, and the front of his shirt grew damp with her tears.

Finally, she drew back and lifted her face to his.

Whatever she'd been about to say was lost as their eyes locked.

Heath knew it wasn't just business bringing him over here tonight, or her grief keeping him here, to comfort her. It was also the developing attraction between them, which went far beyond the physical and the intellectual, reaching down inside him and grabbing his heart. An attraction that had him wanting to be part of her and the kids' life from this day forward. That had him wanting to bend his head to hers and kiss her. Not just once, he thought, as his lips sought and found hers, but again and again and again....

Claire hadn't meant to find comfort in Heath's strong arms. The tenderness in his embrace—the empathy mixed with desire in his kiss—had her kissing him back, more and more passionately, until it was either let things progress, or stop...while they still could.

Wary of the twins upstairs, perhaps not even asleep yet, she tensed.

Getting the message, Heath reluctantly slowed, then leaned back.

"The pitfalls of romancing a woman with children," she said breathlessly.

"Or the benefit," he replied quietly, taking in the longing in her eyes, which matched that in his heart. "Because when we make love again, and we will, it won't be an impulse. It will be because you've thought it through and mean for it to happen."

And once it did, Heath thought, there would be no turning back for either of them.

"ANY CLOSER TO RESOLVING the situation regarding the trust for Claire Olander's niece and nephew?" Orrin Webb asked Heath the next day, over lunch.

He looked at his boss. "Using the mineral rights as a source of income is out."

"What about the Wagner Group? Any luck there?"

"They're interested and could be, I think, persuaded to buy the Red Sage, given a little time and careful, committed negotiation."

"I hear a 'but' in there."

"Claire Olander is not crazy about the idea."

"Ms. Olander is not crazy about anything other than making a go of it herself, and you and I both know what the chances of that are."

Just because it was a long shot didn't mean it wouldn't happen, Heath thought, aware that no one was hoping Claire would pull off a last-minute miracle more than he was. Then the rest of this would be unnecessary and the two of them could get on with building their relationship.

Directing his mind away from his love life and back to the business at hand, Heath told his boss, "I'm going to keep Ted Bauer interested while Claire takes her last shot at making the business profitable. Or at least shows the potential for it to be so in the very near future."

"And if she fails?"

He tensed. Talking this way felt disloyal, even though they all knew he had a job to do here, and would not be dissuaded from doing it. "There are still a couple of options I haven't pitched that would work in the short run, but not the long."

Orrin looked interested. "Such as?"

Heath shrugged. "Claire can only sell the land if she lets o of all twenty-nine thousand at once. There are no such estrictions on the cottages or office, which are owned by the usiness. Selling even one of the cottages outright would ring in enough of a cash infusion to put the Red Sage in he black for a year."

"Like a time-share?"

"Or permanent residence." For himself, Heath thought. If nd when Claire's business picked up, he could always sell back to her. As long as he didn't profit directly and excessvely, it was a perfectly ethical move.

"And there's another way she could expand...."

He spent the rest of lunch strategizing with Orrin. Toether they tried to figure out how they could make that possbility work in the short time frame they had available, ithout Claire even knowing about it—or worrying over the ostacles involved—until it was nearly a done deal.

"You're putting a lot of effort into helping this young oman out," Orrin said.

"It's my job," he stated.

His colleague's face split in a craggy smile. "Keep telling ourself that," he advised dryly, as they headed back to the ank.

Heath had just settled at his desk when his cell phone ng. It was Claire. He picked up and heard the frantic note her voice. "Oh, Heath," she said, "Thank heaven you're ere! Buzz Aberg's e-mail server is down, and he's been ying to fax me the guest list as well as dietary requirements the guests he's bringing with him on Wednesday. But now y fax has suddenly stopped working altogether. I tried to t it going, but it's making this horrible grinding sound...."

That didn't bode well, Heath thought, recalling how the cover had been yanked off the day before by Henry, and put back on by Heath. He'd assumed, because the ready light was still on and he hadn't seen anything amiss, that there was no damage to the machine. Belatedly, he realized he should have given it a test run just to be sure, instead of assuming all was well.

Live and learn.

"Is your e-mail working?" he asked calmly.

"Yes."

"All right. Have Buzz fax the information to me, here at the bank. I'll scan it and send it over to you via e-mail attachment right away."

Claire exhaled in relief. "You're a lifesaver."

She certainly made him feel like a hero. So did the kids whenever he was around them. "No problem," Heath said casually, aware he was glowing like an idiot, which was ridiculous, since he was partially responsible for her current dilemma.

But Claire was already going on. "I mean it. I owe you for this! How about dinner—tonight?"

Heath grinned, already looking forward to it. "Consider it a date."

A FRESH WAVE OF November rain was threatening when Heath left the bank that evening. He turned his collar up against the cold and thought about the warm and cozy evening ahead. Suddenly, the weather didn't seem so gloomy.

As he'd half expected, Claire and the twins were still in the ranch office when he got back there at six o'clock. For once it didn't look as if the play corner had suffered an explosion f toys. Instead, Heidi and Henry were seated at their small ble, coloring intently.

Henry shot a sheepish look at Heath. Heidi, with her sual curiosity, asked, "Are you going to fix Aunt Claire's x machine?"

It seemed imperative to both twins that he did.

"I'm going to try," he said, already taking off his suit coat d rolling up his sleeves. There were no guarantees. He was financial, not a technical, wizard.

Claire drifted closer. The scent of her lavender perfume ung to her skin and hair. "I've never heard any of my elec- onics make a sound like this one is making," Claire stated, ringing her hands.

Heath could see the fax waiting message flashing on e machine.

"Mind if I give it a try?" he asked.

She shrugged. "Can't do any more damage than has eady been done."

He pressed Print, but the machine made an awful inding sound.

Heath quickly pressed the stop button. "I see what you ean. That is pretty bad."

The twins ducked their heads and got even busier.

Heath loosened his tie. "Got an instruction manual?"

Claire winced. "That's part of the problem—I can't find These machines were always Sven's domain, and I have t to figure out where he put the various manuals."

Heath looked behind the machine for the power cord. Jo worries. I'll just turn it off, unplug it and lift the lid."

Heath revealed the guts of the malfunctioning machine. At first glance, he saw nothing wrong with it. The printer cartridge appeared to be correctly snapped in place. There was a paper jam, however. Puzzled that t paper jam error message hadn't been flashing, Heath ca fully worked the edges of torn paper out of the roll guide inside the machine. Instead of coming off in o rumpled sheet, it ripped off in bits, leaving more fra ments trapped inside.

Henry edged nearer. He'd put on his yellow hard h and handed Heath his play wrench and screwdriver. "Y can use these," he offered.

Heath regarded the "tools" with the same seriousne "Thank you, Henry."

Heidi crowded in close and looked over Heath's otl shoulder. "How come it's not working?" she asked, her sn brow furrowed.

Claire came next. She handed Heath a real toolbox. "J in case," she said.

"Thanks."

Heath had never had such a big audience for someth he wasn't sure he could accomplish. With all eyes upon h he went back to work, drawing out more paper and th tucked into a narrow space in the side of the machine matchbox-size motorcycle. A paper clip. Two rubber ba

"Henry…" Claire sighed.

Heidi immediately jumped to her brother's defense. " was just trying to fix it for you."

Henry ducked his head. "It needed some toys to j with," he mumbled.

It had had that all right, Heath mused as he pulled o Magic Marker, a ballpoint pen, two postage stamps and eraser. Afraid there might be still more, he turned to Cl "Got a flashlight?"

Once she'd handed one over, Heath poked around again. He found a couple more rubber bands and some additional bits of stuck paper. "It seems clear now," he said finally. "Let's give it a try." He plugged the machine back in, replaced the cover and pressed Print.

And miracle of miracles, it actually worked.

"I'M SO EMBARRASSED," Claire told Heath later, as she went about cleaning up the supper dishes after the kids were in bed for the night.

She bent to fit a pan in the lower rack of the dishwasher, while he cleared the table for her.

"I knew Henry had taken the cover off, of course, since I was there when he did it, albeit not paying attention. But it never occurred to me that he or Heidi might put anything in there. I guess it just goes to show how preoccupied I've been with the preparations for the Aberg party."

Heath knew she was nervous about the upcoming Thanksgiving weekend. And with good reason. She had a lot riding on it. What she didn't know yet was that this was not her only option; he had found other ways to potentially save the day.

But figuring this wasn't the optimum time to bring that up, since it wasn't a done deal yet, he temporarily kept mum on the subject.

"Look at it this way." He grabbed a spray bottle and misted the table with kitchen disinfectant. "People with kids always have such interesting stories to tell." He grinned at her. "Now I'll have some, too."

She grinned back at him and shook her head. "I notice you said 'some' stories, as in plural," she teased, shutting the dishwasher door.

Heath pulled her close and bent his head. "I plan sticking around for more."

They kissed in a way that was reminiscent of the nig they'd made love. It was filled with so much promise for th future. Sighing, Claire splayed her hands across his che The intimacy of the touch reminded him of other things.

Her eyes lit up as she felt the pressure growing. "Heath.

He struggled to contain his arousal. Letting his har drop to her waist, he shifted reluctantly, so they were longer touching where he most longed to be. "I know." swallowed. "With the kids upstairs asleep…" It wasn't ha to guess where this conversation was going.

Claire extricated herself from his arms and stepped aw self-conscious color tingeing her cheeks. "I'm just not co fortable with the idea of us being intimate when they sleeping in the next room and could wake up at any mome needing comfort, and barge right in." Regret shone in eyes. "They're confused enough already about everyth that has happened in the last year, the overwhelming lc Even subtle changes upset them so much."

Heath understood. He respected Claire for being sc tune with the twins' needs and feelings. It was the mark a good parent. But she was a woman, too. And she nee to administer to her own needs, as well. She needed tc cared for, in the way only he could care for her.

Ready to take as much time as necessary for Claire to comfortable with the idea of them being together, murmured, "So back to us carving out some time alc where we won't feel like we're in a fishbowl, or have worry about what everyone else will think…" Or conclud prematurely.

Claire's eyes lit up in a way that let him know she had already been privately thinking about that herself, weighing possibilities, wanting even as she remained cautious. Heath understood. Relationships between men and women were complicated affairs, driven by so much more than lust and friendship. Despite his best effort, he had misread signs, taken the future for granted. He didn't want to crash and burn again. On the other hand, he thought determinedly, nothing ventured, nothing gained. Everything within him told him he and Claire were on the brink of something exceptional. To not explore that would be foolish, too...

"Mae is going to babysit the kids on Saturday. I'll be making my monthly trip into Fort Stockton to visit the warehouse store there, plus buy in bulk a lot of the food items we'll need for our weekend guests, including the turkeys." She reached for his hand. "It's probably going to be crazy, with crowds up the wazoo, given that Thanksgiving is now just days away...but if you want to go with me, I could ask Mae if she'll babysit the twins into the evening. Which means the two of us could have a real, adults-only, sit-down-in-a-restaurant dinner, before we returned to the ranch."

"As long as it's a date..." Heath brought her closer for another long, tantalizing kiss, indicative of the kind of passion they could experience again, if only they could find the right time and place.

"It definitely is." She nestled contentedly against him.

"Then we're on," he said.

Chapter Ten

Heath heard the voices the moment he stepped into the ranch house Friday evening.

"It's my turn!"

"No, it's my turn!"

"No, it's *my turn!*" This was followed by a bloodcurdling scream, and then another....

Claire came dashing out into the hall. "Stop! Right now! Both of you!"

Heidi and Henry froze.

She retrieved the toy xylophone they had been fighting over and set it aside.

The twins waited, knowing, it seemed, that they were in trouble. Big trouble, for creating such a ruckus.

Claire put her fingers to her temples in the age-old gesture of a parent who was about to lose her mind.

"Okay. Two-minute time-out for both of you."

"Aw..." The protest rang throughout the hall.

Claire lifted an eyebrow. "Want to make it three?"

The twins fell silent.

"Okay. Henry, you take your time-out on the stairs. Heidi, you sit on the bench at the other end of the hall. Go! Now!"

Reluctantly, they trudged to their assigned places.

Claire took the offending object, opened the front hall closet and set it on the highest shelf, way out of reach. She shut the door, glanced at her watch, waited some more. Heath wandered into the living room and he stood at the window, looking out at the rain coming down in sheets.

Finally, Claire said, "Okay. Time-out is over. I expect you to apologize to each other and to me."

"We're sorry," Heidi and Henry said in unison, doing everything but sticking out their tongues at each other.

"You have to mean it for it to count," Claire said.

They sighed and grew more contrite. "I'm sorry," Heidi repeated, and when Henry apologized, too, they hugged one another.

"Okay." Claire sat down on the stairs. "Let's talk."

The twins settled on either side of her.

"I know you two are bored."

"We want to play outside," Henry said for both of them.

"Well, you can't," Claire decreed bluntly. "Not in a cold November rain."

Two lower lips shot out. Then Heidi got a gleam in her eye. "Can we play hide-and-seek then?" she asked.

Henry wrapped his arm around his twin's shoulder, as if the quarrel between the two had never happened. "Yeah. We want you to play, too, Aunt Claire." They peered into the living room, where Heath was still waiting for the "family conference" to be over. "And Mr. Fearsome, too!"

Heath thrust both hands in the pockets of his jeans, and ambled out into the hall.

Claire slanted a shy look at him. "I'm sure Mr. McPherson has better things to do."

"Actually," he said, flashing her a crooked smile, "I don't."

"Okay, but only for half an hour," Claire advised, in a voice that brooked no disobedience. "Then it's going to be bath and bedtime. Got it?"

The children beamed. They turned and gave each other a clumsy, preschool version of a high five, happy, it seemed, that their hours of weather-induced boredom were over. "Got it!"

"Okay, Mr. Fearsome," Claire said, giving him a grateful smile and a high five of her own. "You're 'it'!"

"YOU LOOK...STRESSED," Heath noted when they met up early Saturday morning outside her SUV.

"It's just hit me, all I have to get done today," Claire said.

Looking rugged and relaxed in a long-sleeved, gray polo shirt and jeans, his thick black hair gleaming in the morning sun, Heath cast an easy smile her way. "Want me to drive?"

You have no idea how much, she thought. "That would be great."

Claire put her going-out-to-dinner clothes in the rear compartment, next to his, then grabbed her briefcase and climbed into the passenger seat.

As they drove off, the twins waved from one of the ranch house windows. Mae stood beside them, smiling and waving, too.

As soon as they were out of sight, Claire reached for her notebook and calculator. At Heath's curious glance, she explained, "I don't know how closely you looked at the fax you forwarded to me, but one of the things Buzz sent me the other day was a list of dietary requirements. So I had to come up with appropriate recipes and a way to separate out the specially prepared foods from the normal selections." She sighed. "I've got no idea how big or small people's appetites are going to be. I certainly don't want anyone to go away hungry. So I'm going to err on the side of too much, figuring if I have leftovers, I can always turn them into soup and sandwiches the next day."

"Sounds smart."

"Plus, there are the six other meals I said I would prepare for his group before they leave the ranch on Sunday morning."

Heath sent her an admiring glance. "That's a lot of work."

Claire's tone grew reflective. "And something I'll be doing a lot of if I can tap into the corporate retreat or family reunion market—which is my hope."

As they hit the open highway, Heath set the cruise control on the Jeep. Claire shifted slightly in her seat so she could take in his craggy profile. Damn, but he was fascinating to look at, not to mention kiss…which was something she hoped they would have a chance to do at leisure at some point during this excursion.

"Do you have enough firepower to cook all that food?" he asked curiously.

Claire made a face, as tension set in once again. Reluctantly, she admitted, "Not in the ranch house kitchen. Fortunately, T.S., the Finglesteins and Wiley have all agreed to let me use the stoves and ovens in their cottages, as well. I'll need them to cook four massive turkeys simultaneously."

"So what's the plan? You'll be running from place to place?"

"More or less." Claire sighed again and held up a hand. "I know. I keep thinking I've bitten off more than I can chew, but then I remind myself how much it's going to help if we get a four- or five-star rating from *Southwestern Living* magazine and a plug on their Web site—and I know it's all going to be worth it." Enthusiasm bubbled up inside her. "I can feel it, Heath. The Red Sage Guest Ranch and Retreat is on the verge of being one of those places you don't want to miss, and when that happens it'll be totally booked year-round!"

It appeared her enthusiasm was contagious. He reached over and squeezed her hand in encouragement. "I'll help as much as I can. I'm not much of a chef, but I can follow directions pretty well."

"I appreciate it." Claire paused, thinking how much her life had changed since Heath had entered it, wishing he weren't driving so she could kiss him now. She contented herself by curling her fingers around his biceps, stroking tenderly. "Although I have to say, I don't know how I'm ever going to repay you."

His muscles warming beneath her grip, he glanced at her. "That's the beauty of dating me," he drawled. "You don't have to."

The assumption in his dark-blue eyes made her catch her breath. "Are we dating?" As in an official ongoing thing…?

His mind made up, Heath said, "Starting tonight we are."

"I DON'T KNOW HOW YOU'VE maintained your good cheer," Claire told Heath when they pulled up in front of his town house at five o'clock that evening.

The day's shopping had been a nightmare of long lines, staggering costs that put a huge dent in the guest-ranch books, and endless preholiday traffic.

"Easy," Heath said. As he got out of the SUV and went around to the cargo area, where the four fresh turkeys that they had just picked up from the organic butcher were stowed. "I just kept looking forward to tonight." He picked up two turkeys. Claire took two grocery bags of items that needed refrigeration. They carried them inside to Heath's empty refrigerator, stowed them, and went back for more. It took some doing, but eventually they managed to fit it all in. The cargo area of her SUV, however, was still packed tight with everything from soap and toilet paper to fresh fruits and vegetables.

Unfortunately, because Heath had left his own vehicle back at the ranch, it was all they had to drive this evening.

"Our restaurant reservations are at six-thirty," Heath said as they went back into his elegantly appointed home. He paused at the bottom of the staircase. "I'd like to hit the shower before we go."

The restaurant he had chosen was the best five-star establishment in the area. Claire hadn't been to a steak house that nice since she had stopped working as a marketing rep, two years before. She was a little nervous about what it all meant. Was this what life would be like, dating Heath? Or was he simply going all-out because it was their first official date and he wanted it to be memorable?

"Me, too," she said. She needed the time to take off her frazzled career-woman hat and slip into a mood that was a lot more relaxed and conducive for romance.

He paused. "Everything you need should be in the guest bath."

Her heart began to race. "Thanks."

"I'll take the other. Unless," he murmured, "you'd prefer a bubble bath. In which case, you'll want to use the whirlpool tub in the master bathroom."

A bubble bath sounded heavenly, but the thought of lounging around like that in the tub he used every day…or had when he was still living here…was a bit too disconcerting.

In all likelihood it would make her want to skip dinner and just invite him into the tub with her, to see if their previous encounter had been every bit as wonderful as she recalled.

Telling herself the lovemaking would come later, when the time was right, Claire shook her head. "A shower will be just fine."

Heath carried her garment bag up for her, and she took it from there, luxuriating in the warm spray. Afterward she arranged her curls into an upswept do that perfectly complemented her black cocktail dress. She accessorized her outfit with a simple gold necklace with a crescent moon dangling from the chain, and matching earrings.

And it was only when she went back to the garment bag to pull out her shoes that she realized she had a problem.

HEATH KNEW THE MOMENT he met up with Claire in the living room that something was wrong.

It couldn't be her hair or her jewelry—both were perfect. It couldn't be her dress. She radiated sexiness and sophistication in the clingy black fabric that draped her slender curves like a lover's caress. Nor did he think it was her stockings—they were black and sheer and made the most of her showstopping legs.

She groaned in dismay when his glance dropped lower, then stopped at her feet. "I look ridiculous, don't I?" she said.

Not the word he would have chosen. Although perhaps appropriate, given that she had on one black sling-back pump and one high-heeled, black Mary Jane.

"It could be worse," he teased. "At least you have one right shoe and one left shoe."

"Ha ha." She looked down at her feet, shook her head. "The problem is, the only other shoes I have with me are my cowgirl boots."

Heath shrugged, sliding hands into the pockets of his black suit. "I think you look fine. More than fine."

Claire rolled her eyes. "Uh-huh. Do we have time to stop at a shoe store before we go to the restaurant?"

"Sure. There's one on the way."

Claire pressed a hand over her heart in relief. "Thank heaven."

Heath thought she was a knockout even with mismatched shoes. He knew the eye of every unattached man in the place would be on her tonight. Lucky for him, she was his date.

Unable to resist, he teased, "You might start a trend, you know."

She regarded him with a sour expression. "Or not."

Once again, Heath drove. They'd gotten about a mile and a half from his place when the SUV sounded an alert. Heath looked down at the dashboard, to find the check engine light flashing.

Not good, he thought. Not good at all.

"Oh, no," Claire groaned.

"When was the last time you had your vehicle serviced?" he asked, hoping this wasn't indicative of something dire. He didn't want anything ruining their precious time together, and having to deal with a major car repair would definitely throw a monkey wrench into the evening.

She was apparently thinking the same thing because her eyes filled with panic. "It was serviced last month. Everything was fine."

And now it wasn't. Heath frowned. "We really shouldn't

drive it with the warning light on." Not far, anyway. The engine could catch fire. It could throw a rod, blow a piston....

Claire bit her lip. "Where could we take it at six-fifteen on a Saturday night?"

As far as Heath was concerned, there was only one option. Although it came with complications he really didn't want this evening.

He switched on the left turn signal. "My ex-brother-in-law has an auto shop not far from here. We'll go there."

Claire blinked. "Ex-brother-in-law?" she repeated, as if she couldn't have heard correctly.

Heath had a sinking feeling at the look on her face. Maybe he should have mentioned the fact that he'd been married. "Yeah," he said, wishing he could erase that entire chapter of his life, save for his close relationship with his ex-wife's family. "I'm divorced," he stated, looking Claire right in the eye. "Have been for a couple of years."

DIVORCED. The word echoed over and over in Claire's head. Too late, she realized she had never asked about his marital status. When she'd heard via the Summit grapevine that he was single, and witnessed for herself his desire for a family of his own, she had just assumed he had never been married. That he was as untested in the connubial bliss department as she. Instead, he had tried matrimony and gotten out. That knowledge sent her spinning off on yet another tangent. What had happened to end the relationship?

Her thoughts were still awhirl when Heath turned into the parking lot of Bubba's Garage. The closed sign was already on the front door, but the lights were on, and Claire could see a husky guy with a shaved head moving around inside.

Heath got out of her SUV and waved at him. The next thing she knew the lone mechanic was coming out to greet them.

"Claire, I'd like you to meet Bubba Granger. Best mechanic around. Bubba, my date, Claire Olander."

The big man slapped Heath on the back. "'Bout time you got back out there," he said cheerfully.

Not the response she would have expected from a former brother-in-law, but perhaps a good sign...?

Heath told Bubba about their problem. "The check engine light just came on. We've got to get back to Summit tonight..."

He nodded, all business. "Better have a look under the hood to see what's going on."

He went back to open up the garage, and called over his shoulder, "Drive it on in. We'll run the diagnostics and see what we come up with."

Feeling a little on edge, Claire paced back and forth, shivering in the cool night air, while Bubba hooked the computer up to her car. Heath phoned the restaurant to let them know they were running late.

He was still on the phone when a Jaguar sedan pulled up. A striking brunette clad in a backless silver dress and Manolo Blahnik shoes stepped out. Eyebrows raised, she gave Claire a long, telling look, then headed straight for Heath. She shook her head as if coming upon a mirage. "I thought it was you."

And yet, Claire thought, there was something distinctly unpleasant in her undertone.

Heath's expression remained impassive. "Gina."

She continued to study him with what seemed like a lot of repressed anger. "I thought you'd left Fort Stockton," she stated.

"I'm still trying to sell my townhome," he replied cordially.

Hello! Claire thought. *I'm still here.* But Heath wasn't looking at her. Gina, however, was. Not in a way that made Claire comfortable.

"Aren't you going to introduce me?" the woman said.

"Gina, Claire. Claire, Gina."

Another twist of the dagger. "I'm Heath's ex-wife," Gina said smoothly. "And you are…?"

"His girlfriend," Claire said, before she could stop herself.

Gina's elegantly plucked brows lifted even higher. "I hope you know what you're in for," she drawled. "Romantic, this guy is not."

Bubba hurried out to join them. He glared at his sister, as if silently telling her to knock it off, then turned back to Heath and Claire. "It's a faulty sensor," he declared. "Perfectly safe to drive. Just take it into the dealership when you get home. They'll replace it, no problem. Should even be under warranty."

Claire breathed a big sigh of relief. "Thank you so much."

"Bubba, I owe you." Heath shook his hand.

"You kidding me?" the man said with heartfelt affection. "I *owe* you, man. Big time."

Heath looked at Gina. "Nice to see you again," he said smoothly.

"Wish I could say the same," she retorted bitterly, earning another reprimanding glare from her brother.

Heath took Claire's hand. "If we still want a table, we better get going," he said.

Chapter Eleven

"You want to tell me what that was all about?" Claire asked, when they were seated in the elegant ambience of the upscale steak house.

"I helped Bubba get the small-business loan that he used to start his own garage," Heath said.

She wrapped her fingers around her wineglass. "I meant with Gina."

He winced. "Obviously, she doesn't like me very much."

Claire waited for him to go on. Eventually, he did.

"She feels I let her down."

Claire read the guilt in his expression. She had a hard time reconciling that emotion with the inherently chivalrous man she knew. "Did you?"

He sat back in his chair with a frown. "In the sense that I was never romantic enough for her, yes. Gina wanted every day to be something out of a fairy tale. She didn't like it if I had to work late, or take important customers out for meals. She was upset that I wanted children, which she didn't, even though that was something we had discussed before we ever got engaged, and had supposedly agreed upon."

"So she said she would give you children and then reneged?"

Heath nodded. "She had second thoughts about ruining her figure with a pregnancy."

Not exactly a romantic view of childbirth, Claire thought. But it seemed to fit the striking woman she had met tonight. Claire studied the hurt expression on Heath's face. "How long were you married?"

"Seven years."

That, she hadn't expected. "A long time."

"Yes." He nodded, taking a sip of his wine. "It was."

Claire supposed that fit. Heath was a man who took his responsibilities seriously. Marriage, for him, like his job at the bank, would be at the top of the list. "How did you end up marrying her in the first place?" she asked.

He shrugged. "We were young. We both grew up in the poorest area of the county. Our families had trailer homes side by side. Gina's mom died when she was a kid and she was very enamored of my mother's talents as a hairstylist. I didn't have a dad—he took off before I was born and was never heard from again—so I gravitated toward Gina and Bubba's father." Heath's tone became somber. "He was a good, salt-of-the-earth kind of guy who worked on air-conditioning systems for a living. Health problems left him unemployed for months at a time, so they were always in the ditch financially. My mom worked hard, but she wasn't one for putting any money aside for a rainy day, and it seemed like we were always one step shy of financial ruin, too."

"That sounds tough."

Heath helped himself to a bacon-wrapped sea scallop, with apricot chutney. He cut into it and offered her a bite off his fork. In turn, she offered him a taste of her lobster bisque.

"It showed me what I didn't want," he continued, his blue

eyes darkening. "Gave me the impetus to win scholarships and go to college and work like hell when I got out, so I would never be living hand-to-mouth the way we'd had to most of the time."

It was clear the experience had impacted him emotionally as well as intellectually. It made her understand why he was such a focused-on-the numbers kind of guy. "Did Gina go to college, too?" Claire asked curiously.

It was apparent from the clothes she was wearing that his ex had also done well for herself financially.

Heath waited until the waiter had cleared the appetizers and set their salads in front of them before he continued. "She dropped out midway through her junior year to work full-time at a mall dress shop. She wanted to spend money on clothes, not tuition and books. She figured I'd make a good enough living for both of us. It was just sort of understood that we would marry as soon as I graduated from college, and we did."

Claire thought about how young they had been. At twenty-one, she had been nowhere near ready for marriage. She admired Heath for taking on so large a commitment at such an early age. "So how did it all fall apart?" she asked gently.

"The truth is, things were never all that good between us, but we hung in there because we had common goals—a better life, a nice home of our own, cars… Not to mention paying off our student loans."

"And you achieved all that."

"Within five years, yes."

"But then the trouble started."

He nodded. "We had been arguing about whether or not to start a family, or move to a more exclusive neighborhood.

Then I turned down a job with a bank in New York City. I went for the interview, and realized I just didn't want to live in the Northeast. I love the Lone Star State. Texas is my home. I knew I wouldn't be a multimillionaire if I worked here, but I'd be able to buy everything I wanted and needed, take care of my mom financially—which I did until she died a couple of years ago—and still save for my future." He signed pensively. "That wasn't what Gina wanted. She yearned to go far away and never look back. I couldn't do that. Didn't want to do that. The rancor between us escalated until we finally divorced, by mutual consent. Anyway, she's been married twice since, and managed to elevate her bank accounts both times." He paused. "I wish her well. I wish her happiness."

Claire didn't think Gina was ever going to get it, not with those values. But her estimation of Heath grew. He'd weathered an acrimonious divorce and hadn't let it make him bitter. Instead, he seemed as eager to embark on a relationship with her as she was with him. Life was looking up.

IT WAS NEARLY TEN by the time Claire and Heath left the steak house. "I better check in with Mae, let her know we're going to be a little later than expected," Claire said, as soon as they got back to Heath's townhome. She wished they had more time to be together, but she would just make do with what they did have.

"Oh, thank goodness you called," Mae said. "I was just looking at the weather report. There's heavy fog in the mountains between here and Fort Stockton. It's not supposed to dissipate till midmorning tomorrow. You really shouldn't try to drive back until then."

Claire was torn between elation—more time with Heath!—and worry. "The twins—"

"Had a great day playing with my grandkids, and are now sound asleep. They'll be fine, Claire. I promise. I'll stay here with them, and you keep safe. Don't start home until nine tomorrow morning."

Mae's advice made sense. Driving *would* be treacherous. Claire ended the call, then filled Heath in.

He took the news with the same ease he always showed.

Claire shook her head in wonderment, thinking back over the evening's travails and triumphs. "I'm not sure if this is the worst date ever, or the best," she teased.

He flashed her a crooked grin and leaned against the banister in the foyer. "What do you mean?"

Claire looked down at her footwear. "Well, it started out bad, with mismatched shoes and car trouble, an unexpected run-in with your ex-wife, and a dinner reservation we almost missed."

"Kind of like Murphy's Law of Dates." His dark brows drew together in mock seriousness.

"Exactly." Deciding the time had come to ditch the mistake in footwear, Claire stepped out of her shoes and padded toward him in her stocking feet. The added difference in their height made her feel small and dainty. "But then the car problem turned out to be little more than a nuisance, I decided the shoes didn't matter, our dinner was absolutely wonderful, and now I've just got an excuse to stay out all night."

Claire twirled around happily, spread her arms and dipped in a small, playful curtsy. She felt like a princess who had just been let out of her turret—on an evening pass.

"Can't say I object to that," Heath murmured, looking every bit as delighted as she was by the unexpected turn of events.

He planted his hands on her shoulders, she splayed hers across the solid warmth of his chest. "It's kind of like the date that never got started, initially, but now can't seem to end."

Heath's eyes gleamed with mischief. "We could say good-night if we wanted." He inclined his head. "Part company."

Claire's breath stalled in her chest, and she tingled in anticipation of another way they could go. Especially now that they had all night. "Is that what you want?" she asked softly.

Holding her gaze, he shook his head and let his hands slide down her arms to her wrists, using the leverage to draw them closer still. "I'd like to cherish every second of this unexpected extension of our time together."

They stood facing each other, a scant half inch apart. "Me, too."

Deliberately, he drew her even closer, so their bodies were touching intimately. Then his palms were framing her face and he was lifting it to his. "So what do you want to do next?"

Claire didn't even have to think. Throwing caution to the wind, she pressed her lips to his. His body tautened, and then all was lost in the searing heat and intensity of the kiss. His lips were hot, sensual and persuasive, and Claire kissed him with growing passion.

Heath was everything she wanted in a man. He was strong, smart, sexy. As tough as he was tender. As his tongue swept her mouth, laying claim again and again, she knew she had only been half living until now. He made her want to experience life and pleasure fully. He made her want to take the time to make love and be loved, and she welcomed what was coming....

Heath had expected this to happen. He'd known after the first time they were together that other occasions would follow. He hadn't expected to be so emotionally involved so fast, but as he felt the eager surrender of Claire's body, pressed against his, he knew he was in this all the way. Something happened when they were together. Maybe it was simple chemistry. Maybe it was love. Maybe this was what it felt like when two people were meant to be together for the rest of their lives. He didn't know.

What he was sure of was that Claire fascinated him, had done so from the first moment they'd laid eyes on each other. She exasperated him. Drove him crazy with desire. Made him feel he could tell her anything. Everything. Made him feel as if, together, they could accomplish whatever they dreamed of....

Which was why it was so easy to sweep her into his arms and carry her up the stairs, down the hall to the master suite. Heart pounding, he set her next to the bed. She moaned, a helpless little sound that sent blood rushing to his groin. Senses swimming, he kissed her again, putting everything he had into it, determining that this night would be every bit as memorable as it deserved to be.

Still kissing her, he eased the zipper of her dress down. Pushed the fabric off her shoulders.

She was wearing a sexy little wisp of a black bra that barely contained her breasts. He could see her pale pink nipples jutting against the lace. He pushed her gown lower, and discovered not the panty hose he'd found the last time he made love to her, but a garter belt, stockings and tiny panties every bit as sheer and provocative as the bra.

Groaning at how beautiful she looked in her lingerie, he pushed her dress to the floor, and, trembling, she stepped out of it.

"My turn," Claire said softly. Every bit as willing to please, she tugged off his jacket, undid his tie, unbuttoned his shirt.

She eased the cloth away, let it flutter to the floor next to her dress, then ran her hands over his chest, exploring the flat male nipples, finding the indentation of his waist, his navel.

He shuddered when her hands went to his fly.

He caught her wrist, held it tight. "Maybe that should wait." He already wanted her so badly…

"No way." She undid his belt, drew the zipper down, then his pants. "If I'm in my undies, you have to be, too," she teased, running her palm over his arousal.

Feeling as if he might explode then and there, he took off his shoes, pants and socks. Then, aching with the need to savor and possess, he took control once again.

Her lips were wet and swollen from his kisses, her hair tousled, her cheeks pink. They'd hardly begun and already her body was primed and ready for him. Aware that nothing had ever seemed as right, as having her here with him, he kissed her again, lazily at first, then hotter, harder, deeper.

Every bit as caught up in their lovemaking as he was, Claire moaned and opened her mouth to the pressure of his, tangling her tongue with his, using the sweet suction of her lips to draw him in even farther. Her hands caressed his back, his spine, his buttocks, his thighs, before starting at his shoulders and provocatively making their way down all over again.

Not to be outdone, he bent her backward over one arm, held her there, while his head dropped to explore the exquisiteness of her breasts. Her nipples were tight little buds of desire. He explored them through the sheer lace of her bra, laving, suckling, caressing, until she was moaning, lifting her hips.

Aware he'd never wanted a woman more, Heath lowered her to the bed. Took off her bra. Unhooked the garters. Pulled her panties down, then, with the light, sure stroking of his hands, got her to part her legs for him.

She was so beautiful, so sleek and feminine. Her breath hitched when he eased his thumb back and forth over her soft, slick core. Succumbing, Claire shut her eyes, let her head fall back. She gave in to the sensation, arching her spine when he repeated the tender assault with lips and tongue. Reveling at her responsiveness, he explored the whole of her femininity, caressing, stroking, teasing, moving his fingers inside to stretch and torment, until they were wet with her essence. She bucked upward, stretching her toes and urging him on, whimpering softly all the while, and then climaxed with such intensity it was all he could do not to join her in ecstasy.

"No fair," Claire whispered, as she slowly caught her breath. She clasped his head in her hands as he made his way back to her mouth. "I wanted to wait for you."

Perspiration beaded her body, moisture coated her inner thighs. "But since I didn't…" With the sultry smile of a satisfied woman, she pushed him flat on his back, stripped off his boxer briefs. "It's my turn…to be in charge…"

It sounded good, except… "Not sure how long you have," he gasped. He loved the way she looked, so alluring, so ravished, so completely and utterly his….

"As long as I want," Claire murmured as he trembled with the effort to hold back his own response.

Claire had never been an adventurous lover. Never had the confidence to really go after what she wanted in bed. But with Heath it was different. When he looked at her in that reverent, unsettling way, he made her feel like the most beautiful woman on earth. Which was why it was so easy to let her hair drift over his stomach, to glide lower, to explore his body with the same loving intensity he had shown exploring hers. His muscles were hard, his skin satin, his chest hair crisp and curly. He smelled like soap and cologne and the provocative musk of arousal. His sheer masculinity heightened her senses and drove her to explore, touching, stroking, caressing…

"My turn again," Heath said. Swiftly trading places with her, so she was on her back, he draped himself over her, easing between her legs, as if he'd done it a million times before.

Quivering, she wound her arms and legs around him and declared, "*Our* turn."

Uttering a soft, triumphant sound, Heath pressed against her and kissed her hard. Kissed her until there was no denying what either of them wanted. Desire took over, making her feel hot, inside and out. And then he was lifting her hips, parting her legs even farther, and they were gloriously, inevitably one.

"This is meant to be," Heath whispered, as he penetrated her a little more. And then more, until he was in as deep as he could go. Sliding out, slowly, slowly back in, with each deliberate, passionate movement possessing her all the more. Toes curling, she clung to him, enjoying the wild ride. When she would have hurried him along, he held back even more, making her understand what it was to savor every sensation, to throb with the need to let go completely. Hands cupping her bare bottom, he lifted her a little higher. She tightened around him, pulling him deeper still, until there was no more thinking, only feeling, only wanting, only this incredible mounting passion and the sensation of sharing one heart and soul. Of moving toward a single goal.

Then all reason fled, and they were free-falling into an oblivion that was as sweet and satisfying as anything either had ever felt.

FOR LONG MINUTES following, aftershocks coursed through their bodies. This time, though, as Heath rolled onto his back, taking her with him, Claire was in no hurry to draw away.

She lay spent, her head on his chest, his body taut and warm beneath her. Heath tightened his arms around her and pressed a kiss into her hair in a way that made her feel even more loved. "That," he said, "was something." The low, husky tone of his voice demonstrated that he was just as affected by what had transpired as she.

Claire sighed contentedly, knowing she had never felt so safe, so treasured. "Wasn't it?"

She had come here hoping they would have another chance to make love. She had expected doing so would be full of excitement and physical thrills. She hadn't expected Heath to rock her world emotionally, but that was exactly what he had done.

He had shown her how to let her guard down. How to relax and enjoy their time together as thoroughly as possible, how to open up to the possibilities of life and love. He'd made her want to explore the sensual side of herself, and share her life with him. And that was a revelation, too.

She hadn't figured that kind of commitment was in the cards for her.

She'd discovered that her heart had very different ideas, when it came to Heath and the future....

He had seemed similarly affected when they were making love, and now, as they continued to hold each other close.

He kissed her shoulder, the nape of her neck, the lobe of her ear, before returning with slow deliberation to her mouth. "How much of a sports aficionado are you?" he murmured, after another leisurely kiss.

"Not sure," she said dryly. "Why?"

He trailed a hand down her arm. "I was just wondering how you might feel about an 'instant replay.'"

She shifted onto her stomach, draped one of her legs between his and propped her chin on her fist. "Actually," she drawled, "I get bored doing the same things over and over again. So…" She threw back the sheet and climbed astride him.

Heath's eyes lit up. "You may have a point there," he murmured. "There's always something to be gained by trying something new."

Claire laughed softly. She dropped down so her breasts rubbed against his chest, and delivered another languid kiss. "So what do you say we try…this?" She rose slightly on her knees, then dropped down again, the lower half of her caressing the lower half of him.

He groaned at the pleasurable friction, and then, gripping her waist, made them one again. "I'd call it the perfect end to the perfect date."

"Mrs. Lefman said you couldn't come home last night 'cause there was fog in the mountains!" Henry announced, at ten-thirty the next morning, when Claire and Heath finally walked in the front door.

Score one for low visibility, Claire thought. "That's right." And that little twist of fate had solidified her and Heath as a couple. Not that he'd actually said anything to her to verify this. But it was evident in the way he looked at her, in the way he'd kissed her this morning before they'd headed out the door. Like someone in love...

Which was, coincidentally, exactly the way she had kissed him, Claire thought, casting a sideways glance at Heath.

"How come there was fog in the mountains?" Heidi asked, drawing Claire back to the present.

"Because of all the storm fronts that have been coming through the last few days," she explained.

"Are they all gone now?" the little girl asked.

The clear blue sky up above suggested they might be. Unfortunately, weather reports on the radio today indicated otherwise. "We're going to have nice weather for the next three days, and then it's going to rain again on Wednesday evening."

Just in time for Buzz Aberg and all the Thanksgiving guests to start arriving.

But Claire plastered a bright smile on her face so the kids wouldn't pick up on her worries.

After the twins helped the adults unload the SUV and put everything away, Claire suggested they all take advantage of the good weather while it lasted. Heidi and Henry beamed when she agreed to let them put seed in the bird feeders scattered around the property, and they could barely contain their delight when Heath suggested a picnic lunch to take with them.

The four soon set off under cloudless skies, and a balmy sixty-degree temperature. Henry insisted on wearing his yellow hard hat and toy tool belt, in case any of the feeders needed fixing. Heidi wore her play baby carrier, with Sissy tucked against her chest. The twins led the way down the familiar hike and bike path, Claire and Heath taking up the rear.

"I had a message from Wiley Higgins on my voice mail," Claire said. "Apparently, he still hasn't signed that other ranch. He wants one more shot at looking for oil on the Red Sage."

"You could put him off until next Monday," Heath suggested.

Claire darted him a glance. Why would she want to do that?

"See if things work out with *Southwestern Living* magazine the way you want before you shut that door entirely," he explained.

Claire stiffened at the notion that Heath was not one hundred percent behind her efforts to save the business the old-fashioned way, via ingenuity, plain hard work and superior salesmanship. Ninety-nine point nine percent was not good enough!

Unable to conceal the layer of ice that had come into her tone, she said, "Whether things work out with Buzz Aberg or not, I'm not taking Wiley up on his offer."

Silence fell between them as they walked along the trail. She could feel his disapproval. And although Claire now understood why—no doubt Heath was making some comparison between his mother's refusal to act responsibly and spare his family the pain of near financial ruin, and Claire's own desire for a happy ending via a timely magazine endorsement of the guest ranch—that did not make it any easier for her to bear.

Claire wanted Heath to support her without question. To believe as she did. Negative energy could only bring her, and the business, down.

Heath took her elbow when an uneven stretch caused her to momentarily lose her footing. "Have you thought about getting a small-business loan to renovate the barn into a party facility?"

Claire leaned into him briefly, then moved away. "A small-business loan requires ten percent down, minimum. I don't have it. Liz-Beth, Sven and I mortgaged everything there was in order to build the cottages." Which meant she was still cash poor. Even more so after yesterday's spending spree...

Heath shrugged off her concern. "That's not an uncommon problem for people wanting to start or expand their own businesses. For instance, I helped Bubba, my ex-brother-in-law, put together some outside money from investors so he could apply for the loan that enabled him to start his garage."

When it came to money, things were never as easy as they seemed. However, Claire tried to keep an open mind about what he was proposing.

Heath supervised while the twins filled a low-standing bird feeder, then helped them put the lid back on.

"What did Bubba have to give in exchange?" Claire asked eventually.

"A guaranteed return on par with a good mutual fund. And he had to report to a supervisory board, comprised of said investors."

A chill went down Claire's spine. "What does that mean—'report'?"

Heath met her gaze with equanimity. "He had to meet with them bimonthly and have their approval for all fiscal decisions."

Claire exhaled, her frustration mounting. "So if he wanted to purchase something, or hire employees..."

"Bubba had to run it by them first," Heath said pragmatically.

Claire scowled as the twins raced on ahead to a clump of blooming red sage. "That sounds like a major headache."

Heath shook his head. "They were all sound businesspeople. They provided valuable input to Bubba on everything from lease options to building codes to the employee handbook for his company."

"So, in other words, Bubba's business was no longer his own—at least not the way he first envisioned it," Claire said sarcastically. "And he paid a lot higher interest rate for that borrowed down payment than if he'd had a regular bank loan."

"Yes. But given the fact he didn't have the collateral to obtain a regular loan, and the investment was high risk, it was a fair exchange. And as I said, Bubba benefited from all the advice. In any case, he paid those start-up funds back within a year, and once that was done, resumed full ownership and control of his business. As you would, I'm sure." Heath paused a short distance away from the twins, who were busy picking red blossoms from the bush, to take back to the ranch house. "It's a little late, but I could put something together for you before the December first deadline."

Claire shook her head. "I can't see myself answering to anyone, Heath, no matter how well-intentioned." She couldn't believe he would ask her to do that, either. "And that goes double for any board of advising investors."

It was Heath's turn to frown. "At least think about it," he urged, looking intently into her eyes.

Claire turned away. "I can't, Heath. I'm sorry," she told him softly, doing her best, once again, to ignore the palpable disappointment in his expression. "I'd rather give up on the guest ranch entirely than do something like that."

HEATH LET THE SUBJECT drop because he didn't want to spoil the end of their weekend together. His silence, however, did not mean he had changed his view about the kind of preemptive action Claire needed to take.

Knowing she had no intention of changing her mind, he made his own plans for protecting the business portion of the twins' trust, and acted appropriately under the circumstances.

He knew he would have to talk to Claire about his plans. He would do so at a time when all her other options had been exhausted and she was likely to at least listen to him.

In the meantime, he had to enlist help of his own. And by the time he walked into the Summit restaurant early Monday morning, Ginger Haedrick was already there, talking on her cell phone.

She lifted her hand in a wave. He took a seat opposite her as she concluded her business conversation.

"What is so important that you're missing the breakfast buffet at the Red Sage and meeting me here in town instead?" Ginger asked, looking every bit the Type A woman in her olive-green wool suit.

Leave it to her to cut straight to the chase. "I have a property I want you to break down and appraise for me," he said. "And I want it done quietly."

"Okay. Any particular reason why?" She got out a yellow pad and pen and started taking notes.

Heath hedged, wary of revealing too much. "I may be interested in purchasing a portion of it."

Ginger paused in obvious confusion. "I thought you weren't interested in buying anything until your townhome in Fort Stockton sold."

"That's still my preference." He sipped his coffee.

"Is the property you want me to investigate on the market?"

"No."

Ginger sat back. "Okay, now you've got me fascinated."

Briefly, Heath explained his idea.

Recognition dawned in her eyes. "Claire knows nothing about this, right?"

Heath felt a flare of guilt, which he suppressed. "I'm hoping it won't come to this," he stated candidly.

"But you'll be ready to act quickly if it does?"

No sense pretending. Heath nodded.

Ginger tapped her pen on the pad. "Why don't you just tell Claire what you've got in mind?"

"A lot of reasons," he insisted.

"I'm listening."

Aware that Ginger was not likely to undertake such a covert action unless he was straight with her, Heath said, "I respect Claire's ability to dream. I could never do what she has done, starting a guest ranch from scratch."

Ginger understood, even if at heart she was more like Claire than Heath. "You're more a company guy."

"Right. I like working for a big bank, having that kind of security."

"And Claire wants none of it."

"For her, working for someone else is not an acceptable option."

"Which is why she nixed the idea of selling out to the Wagner Group," the real-estate agent said thoughtfully.

"You heard about that?"

She shrugged. "I'm still trying to sell the VP, Ted Bauer, on the area. Although personally, I think Claire's a fool for not letting Wiley Higgins hunt for oil on her property. Either option is money in the bank."

"I'm trying to increase the monetary return on the twins' trust in a way that is acceptable to all."

Ginger scoffed. "You keep telling yourself that," she teased. "At least until you can own up to the real reason behind your actions."

Heath paid for breakfast and told Ginger he needed the information he'd asked her to get for him by Sunday afternoon at the very latest.

"No problem." She walked with him to the parking lot. "I had no plans for the Thanksgiving weekend, anyway."

Heath paused next to her car. He knew what it was like to have nowhere to go on holidays. Damn lonely. "I thought Claire invited you to the ranch, for dinner there."

Ginger waved off the invitation with a decided lack of enthusiasm. "I declined. Homey gatherings aren't my thing. But y'all have a good time, and I'll meet up with you—" she lightly touched Heath's arm "—on Sunday afternoon, to go over the figures and, if need be, write up a bid."

Heath wished Claire had more time. He wanted her to succeed on her own, without any help from him. But he knew she might not, so, for everyone's sake, he had to be prepared to make a last-minute save, even if she resented him for it.

Ginger studied him, taking in the ambivalence he was unable to hide. She leaned in confidentially and stated, "Don't look so conflicted. You are *not* stabbing Claire in the back by doing this."

Then why, Heath wondered, as he and Ginger said a cordial goodbye, did it feel as if he was?

Chapter Twelve

Claire stood on Main Street, barely believing her eyes. Heath and Ginger Haedrick were walking out of a coffee shop together engaged in what appeared to be a very intimate conversation…and an even more emotional goodbye.

Since when had the two of them become such good friends? she wondered.

And why hadn't Heath mentioned he was seeing Ginger this morning?

Was he back to looking at property? Did that mean he wanted to leave his cottage at the Red Sage?

If that was the case, perhaps he thought it might be too uncomfortable to stay there if she didn't have all her ducks in a row financially by December first. Which meant he'd have to make a decision about protecting the twins' fiduciary interests.

Or was he frustrated because she'd been too busy caring for the twins and making additional preparations for the Thanksgiving weekend to find time for him last night?

Claire had no answers. All she did know was that she didn't want it to look like she was spying on him, so she ducked into Callahan's Mercantile & Feed, intent on running the errand that had kept her in Summit after dropping off the kids in the preschool car pool.

The proprietress, Hannah Callahan Daugherty, came toward her, her adopted daughter, Isabella Zhu Ming, toddling beside her. "Here for all those hurricane globes and candles?" Hannah asked cheerfully.

Claire nodded. She had ordered fifty of them in advance of a winter storm that was now making its way across the country. She crossed her fingers. "I'm really hoping we won't need them."

"It looks like all the snow and ice is going to stay well north of us. All we're going to get are some powerful bands of thunderstorms."

She found little comfort in that. "We could still lose electricity."

"Don't say that!" Hannah held up both hands as if to ward off a jinx. "With all those holiday meals to cook! And the storm due to hit late Wednesday and continue through early Thursday morning. That could be a disaster."

Especially out in the rural part of the county, where she lived, Claire thought. "I'm hoping if I am well prepared we won't need any of this," she stated glumly.

Hannah rang up the purchases, while keeping one eye on two-year-old Isabella, who was sitting on a rug behind the cash register playing with a tower of Lego blocks. "That's the way it goes. If you're not prepared, you can expect disaster. If you go all out to make sure you are prepared, nothing happens."

Which was what Claire was counting on. She had too much riding on this weekend.

She was still ruminating on the weather as she headed

back home. Mae was in the ranch house kitchen when she arrived, making piecrusts that would be baked later in the week. Mrs. Finglestein was helping. "I thought you and your husband would be out birding this morning," Claire said to her guest.

It was a beautiful day, sunny and clear.

The woman smiled. "We're going this afternoon. Right now he's uploading a lot of the video we've shot thus far back to our birding group in upstate New York. They're all a little skeptical at what we've been telling them we've seen thus far so we thought we'd send them proof." She winked. "Be warned, though, you might have a rush of reservations this winter and spring, as a result."

"I'd be happy to host anyone who would like to come," Claire said, as an idea began to form. If only she wasn't so busy with the Buzz Aberg group coming in on Wednesday, she'd get on it right now.

Mae gave her a long look. "Everything okay?"

She pushed the image of Heath and Ginger from her mind. "I'm feeling a little frazzled."

Mae's eyes narrowed. "Looks like more than that to me."

"To me, too," Mrs. Finglestein said, "if you don't mind me saying so."

O-kay. Well, maybe it was time for a second and third opinion on what might or might not be going on. "How well did either of you get to know Ginger Haedrick when she was staying here?" Claire asked casually.

The two women exchanged glances and shrugged.

"She wasn't much for chitchat," Mrs. Finglestein said finally.

Mae agreed. "Unless it was about business. Then you couldn't get her to stop talking."

"Did she ever talk about dating anyone?" Claire could have shot herself the moment the words were out of her mouth.

"Oh, yes," Mrs. Finglestein declared.

Mae lifted a brow, as did Claire.

"She's a 'player,'" the woman explained. "Only goes out with a man if she likes his financial prospects."

Mae nodded. "She's looking for someone who is as vested in the bottom line as she is. Someone who could give her 'the good life,' is how she put it. And given how determined Ginger is, I think she'll get it."

Which could only mean that she was after Heath, Claire thought, her spirits plummeting even more.

"HAVE I DONE SOMETHING?" Heath asked Claire Monday evening. "Are you angry with me?"

Trying not to think how it felt to have competition for the man she had come to think, however foolishly, as all hers, she held the front door for him.

Too late, she realized they had never really laid out any ground rules. Never declared themselves an official couple or vowed to date each other exclusively. Heath hadn't been breaking any rules because there were none to disrespect!

Aware he was still trying to figure out the shift in her mood, she fought back a self-conscious flush. "No," she said stiffly. "Of course not."

He paused in the doorway, suitcase full of clothes in his hand, and gave her a probing look. "Is it going to be a problem, having me bunk under the same roof as you and the twins for the next seven days? Because if it is, I could probably find a room in town."

Near Ginger? "Don't be ridiculous," Claire snapped. "The ranch house is plenty big. And the twins are going to love having you close by."

An enigmatic glint came into his blue eyes. "Then what is it?"

"I saw you today."

"Where?" he asked, moving so near she had to tilt her head back to see his face.

"Leaving the coffee shop with Ginger Haedrick," she blurted.

A flash of guilt and evasiveness crossed his face. "We had a breakfast meeting," he said flatly.

"It's none of my business." Desperate to get out of the closed space, she tried to step by him. He put out a hand to stop her.

"It is your business if you're jealous."

Irritated that he saw so much of her true feelings when she wanted him to see nothing, she huffed. "I'm not jealous!"

"Funny," he murmured, "I could swear otherwise."

Another silence stretched. Crossing her arms beneath her breasts, Claire shivered with a chill that had nothing to do with the room temperature. "Are you dating her?"

Heath did a double take. "Why would you think that?"

Glad she'd been so far off the mark, she avoided his eyes. "We've never said we were exclusive."

Heath clamped both his hands on her spine and brought her close. "Then let me set the record straight," he murmured, dropping his head and delivering a long, passionate kiss that stole her breath. Raking his fingers through her tousled curls, he kissed her again and again, until yearning welled deep inside her. Until she was all too ready to look in his eyes and listen to his soft, husky confession.

"The only woman I am interested in, Claire Olander, the only woman I will ever be interested in," he said, pausing to kiss her again, "is you…"

IT WAS ONLY LATER, as Claire got ready for bed, that she realized Heath had never really answered her question. He'd just kissed her until all her doubts fled.

Then he'd carried the rest of his stuff in.

She'd bidden him good-night after she'd made sure he had settled comfortably into his guest room. Then she'd checked on the twins, who were still sleeping peacefully, and retired to her own room.

Alone, she couldn't help thinking back to the look he'd had on his face when she'd asked him about his breakfast with Ginger. As if he were guilty of holding back something. And that stunned her. Up to now, Heath had been direct in his approach to the situation. He'd told it like it was, at least according to the numbers. Given her options. Let her make her own choices, while still letting her know that at the end of the day if she didn't succeed, something she probably wouldn't like would have to be done about the trust for the twins, in order to protect their inheritance. So what could he be keeping from her now? Why—and how—was he in cahoots with Ginger? Were the two of them already making contingency plans to sell off at least part of the ranch? How was she going to feel if Heath had to be the person to squash her family's dream?

Would she resent him so much that any further romance

would be impossible? Or would she rise above it, and accept the fact that he was only doing his job, just as she was trying like heck to do hers?

Claire turned over on her stomach and buried her face in her pillow.

She had to stop courting failure, even in her most uncertain moments. She had to think positive. Work hard. And make her vision for the ranch a reality.

THE REST OF TUESDAY and most of Wednesday passed in a blur of activity. All the cottages were cleaned and polished. All the prep work that could possibly be done in the kitchen was accomplished. All four mammoth turkeys were washed and made ready to go in the ovens. Stuffing was prepared, vegetables scrubbed and cut up, pies baked.

By the time Buzz Aberg and his family started checking in, around 6:00 p.m. on Wednesday evening, storm clouds were rolling in, the first of several waves of thunderstorms projected over the next few days.

"You're worried, aren't you?" Heath said, when Claire had finally finished settling everyone in, around eight-thirty.

Raindrops spattered as the two of them made their way from the ranch office to the house.

She nodded. "I had planned to have Thanksgiving dinner outside tomorrow, on tables set up in the yard. I'm still hoping to do that, if it's not too muddy and we get a break in the rain—at least for the day."

Heath caught her hand in his and ducked beneath the portico that sheltered the back entrance to the house. "It's going to be okay. I'll be here the entire weekend, ready to assist in whatever way I can."

Claire warmed at the affection in his blue eyes. "My white knight to the rescue?" she teased softly.

Heath grinned. "More than that." He pulled her into the shadows and delivered a steamy kiss that promised so much more than friendship and desire. She looked up, wishing she didn't know what an insatiable lover he was.

If only she didn't have any other responsibilities tonight... If only she was still a single woman with a job that delivered a steady paycheck and a lot fewer hours... She'd be free to spend the entire holiday weekend with Heath, making love whenever, wherever they pleased.

Reading her mind, he traced her lower lip with the pad of his thumb. "Our time will come, before the weekend's over. I promise you that."

"I'm going to hold you to it," Claire whispered back.

They kissed again. Then, aware that Mae was inside, waiting to go home to her own family and responsibilities, they headed inside.

Mae was in the kitchen, taking the last of the pies out of the oven. The rest were cooling on a multilayered restaurant baking rack.

She smiled at Claire. "The twins went to bed about an hour ago. I guess I don't have to tell you they're very excited."

Claire chuckled. "They love a holiday."

"Anyway, unless something comes up, I'll see you on Friday morning, bright and early," Mae said.

Claire nodded. "And thanks for everything."

"No problem." She flashed a smile as she picked up her umbrella and headed out the door.

The kitchen smelled heavenly.

Heath and Claire were alone once again. Though for

how long was anyone's guess. With the guests still getting settled into the various cottages, Claire expected a few more phone calls or even knocks on the door before the evening was over.

"Think it would be terrible of us to cut a small piece out of one of those pies?" she asked Heath, trying to think of another satisfying way to spend the evening together, other than by climbing into her bed and making love all night long. But with storms predicted and the twins just down the hall, that was probably not a good idea.

Oblivious to the passionate nature of her thoughts, Heath studied the array of pies with their flaky golden crusts.

"After all, we've got to have some reward for all the hard work we've been doing," Claire added with a wink. "So…" she splayed her hands over his chest "…got any preferences?"

Heath's muscles hardened beneath her touch. He looked past her. "The mincemeat looks pretty good."

"Then mincemeat it is." Claire cut two pieces, still warm from the oven, and topped both with whipped cream.

She and Heath lounged side by side against the counter, shoulders touching, and enjoyed their pie. No sooner had they finished than they found themselves kissing again, even as thunder rumbled in the background and rain began pelting the ground.

Reluctantly, they drew apart, by unspoken agreement deciding to wait for a better place and time.

"We better check on the twins," Heath murmured as lightning flashed again. The rain came down even harder, followed by reverberating thunder.

Claire took his hand in hers. "You know how they are about storms," she said.

Upstairs, Heath and Claire looked in on Heidi and Henry. To their amazement, despite the rumbling outside, both children were still curled up in their beds, sound asleep. Claire adjusted the covers tenderly, stood there a second longer, then backed out of the room.

Gallant as always, Heath said, "I know you've got an early day tomorrow."

She nodded, wishing she didn't. But given all that was riding on a fabulous Red Sage experience for the Aberg clan, she couldn't afford to be an ounce short on energy. So she kissed Heath again, slowly and sweetly, and retired to her bedroom. She had just climbed beneath the covers when lightning flashed so brightly it lit up the entire sky, and thunder rumbled so hard and close it shook the house.

She dashed to the window, just in time to see the top branches of a live oak tree a hundred feet from the house splinter and catch fire. Then another deafening clap of thunder sounded.

Claire's bedroom door slammed open.

The twins, crying hysterically, ran in, followed swiftly by Heath.

"Get in bed!" Heidi screamed.

"We've got to put the covers over our head!" Henry shouted.

Knowing the only thing that would calm the twins was refuge in her queen-size poster bed, Claire waved them toward it.

Wondering what her guests were making of this fierce storm, and thankful they had not yet lost electricity, she checked to make sure the pouring rain had put out the fire in the tree. After assuring herself that it had, she climbed in after the twins.

"You, too, Mr. Fearsome!" Henry directed.

"You've got to get safe!" Heidi cried.

Heath looked at Claire.

Another clap of thunder sounded, louder and closer than ever.

Claire lifted the covers on the other side. "Hurry," she said.

Clad in striped pajama bottoms and a V-necked T-shirt, Heath climbed in. Before they knew it, Henry was in his arms and had a death grip around Heath's neck. Heidi had done the same with Claire. Heath and Claire found themselves lying side by side, each with a quaking four-year-old draped over their chest.

They soothed them through the duration of the storm, which lasted another fifteen or twenty minutes. Finally, the thunder and lightning went away, and all that was left was the soft, rhythmic sound of falling rain.

"You ready to go back to your own beds now?" Claire asked wryly, aware this wasn't how she'd prefer to spend time in bed with the man next to her.

"Nooo!" the twins shouted in unison. "We want to sleep with you and Mr. Fearsome!"

Claire looked over the top of Heidi's head. Her room was still lit by her bedside reading lamp, so it was easy to see the mixture of compassion and patience in his eyes.

"I'm comfortable," he said. "Henry, you doing okay?"

"Yes." The boy gripped Heath's neck tighter and nestled his face in his shoulder, just as he used to bury his head in the crook of Sven's neck.

Claire asked gently, "Heidi, are you okay?"

The child nodded, then after a second asked, "Aunt Claire, is it thundering in heaven, too?"

As always, the question caught Claire off guard, like a blow to her solar plexus. How to answer that? Finally, she said, "I don't think so, honey."

"But heaven is in the sky!" Heidi protested.

"And thunder and lightning are in the sky," Henry pointed out.

"So Mommy and Daddy must be scared, too," his sister declared.

Claire paused, thinking how best to soothe and reassure them. "Heaven is like the sky," she said finally. "There are fluffy white clouds there. And angels. And lots of good things. The thunderstorms we are having tonight are in a different sky."

The twins stared at her, uncomprehending.

Once again, Claire felt she'd made a mess of things. As if she wasn't cut out for any of this. As if she wasn't strong or gifted enough to be a parent, never mind under these challenging circumstances.

Still, because the twins were depending on her, she tried again. "Where Mommy and Daddy are…the heaven they are in…is a wonderful place."

"With lots of sunshine and red flowers and stuff," Henry guessed.

Claire nodded, then said, as inspiration struck, "It's a lot like this ranch. The heaven they are in has everything they love and cherished in life." *Except the two of you,* she added mentally. "They're very happy there. They are safe. And loved. And warm. You don't have to worry about Mommy and Daddy. They're okay."

"And they're watching over us," Henry recalled.

Claire nodded, the familiar knot of grief in her throat once again. "Every moment of every day," she promised hoarsely.

Half an hour later, the twins were both fast asleep. Claire was getting very drowsy, too. Beside her, snuggled close, too, Heath was already asleep. Both of them still had a child in their arms, and with another thunderstorm approaching—she could hear the rumble in the distance, and see the flashes lighting her window—she decided against waking Heath to try to get the kids back in their own beds.

Better to just go with what was successful, she thought drowsily. And right now, the sensation of familial intimacy was what was working. The image of Heath as daddy figure to the twins, potential life mate and husband to her, was all she needed to have a truly happy Thanksgiving holiday.

Chapter Thirteen

Claire woke to sunlight pouring through the windows.

Heidi was snuggled up next to her in the center of her bed, Henry nestled beside his sister, and Heath lay prone on the far edge of the mattress, sound asleep. Luxuriating for a moment in the cozy feeling of well-being that came after waking from such a deep, restful sleep, Claire turned to study the new man in her life.

Heath took her breath away. He was so gorgeous, with sleep-rumpled black hair, and the stubble of a beard lining his chin. She longed to lean over and kiss him, the way a princess might kiss her prince to waken him. Would have, if they'd been alone...

The fringe of inky-black lashes lifted. Turning slightly, Heath rested his sleepy blue eyes on her. A sexy smile turned up the corners of his lips. "Morning," he whispered.

A thrill raced through her. "Morning," she whispered back.

He nodded at the sleeping darlings between them. "Not how I figured we'd be spending our *second* night together," he murmured with a wink. "But fun just the same."

Claire reached over to link hands with him. "You were great last night." So solid and strong and reassuring.

He tightened his grip. "So were you."

He held her eyes. "How much time do we have before you have to get to work?"

Work. Company. Buzz Aberg and his many guests. She had almost forgotten!

Claire turned to glance at the bedside clock and saw the flashing lights that indicated a power failure. Oh, no…!

They had lost electricity at some point in the night.

And although it had come back on, none of the clocks on the ranch would have the right time.

"We overslept!" She sat up in a rush.

Henry and Heidi snuggled deeper into the covers.

"By how much?" Heath was not wearing his watch, either.

"I've got no idea!" Claire slipped from the bed, suddenly conscious of the fact that she wasn't wearing a bra beneath her long-sleeved pajama T-shirt.

The chilly air of the house made her nipples contract, a fact not lost on Heath, sleepy eyes or not. She grabbed a robe.

But if the alarm had gone off when she'd set it, it would still be dark outside… "I've got to take a shower, get started."

He waved her on, already easing from under the covers. "I'll get cleaned up, too, so I can help."

By the time Claire had swept her damp curls into a clip on the back of her head, and put on a figure-hugging denim skirt and a turtleneck sweater with the Red Sage Guest Ranch logo across the front, the twins were wide-awake and playing on the rumpled covers of her bed.

"We sleeped with both you and Mr. Fearsome last night!" Henry stated, enthralled the way only a four-year-old could be.

"Yeah, we cuddled real good," Heidi noted.

Please don't let them mention this to the guests, Claire

prayed silently, as she adeptly steered the conversation to another topic.

But of course, as luck would have it, they did.

It was, in fact, the first thing the twins talked about when they dashed into the breakfast buffet.

"Henry and Heidi are very frightened of thunderstorms," Claire found herself explaining to Buzz Aberg's entire family and the other ranch guests as she replenished the orange juice dispenser. "To the point they've gotten the idea that the only safe place. when they happen at night, is my bed."

"Yeah," Henry expounded after agreeing to sample some scrambled eggs along with his toast and juice. "We had to invite Mr. Fearsome to come with us, too. So's he wouldn't get kaboomed by the lightning!"

"He didn't *want* to come in with us," Heidi elaborated, "but we made him."

"They were quite unreasonable in their fear," Heath commented to the guests, in a droll tone that elicited knowing expressions and more than a few chuckles.

"Fortunately, Heath was adept at comforting them, as well as a good sport." Claire telegraphed her gratitude to him for that, even as she fought a self-conscious blush.

Speculative looks abounded, along with a few nods of approval.

"Ever thought of becoming a dad?" Mr. Finglestein asked the question that seemed to be on everyone's mind.

"You seem to have a knack for parenting," his wife observed.

Heath locked eyes with Claire. And in that instant, she knew something fundamental was changing. A door to the future was opening. "More and more," he said.

SEVERAL HOURS LATER, Heidi and Henry skidded to a stop just inside the ranch house kitchen, where Mrs. Finglestein and Claire were busy stuffing the four turkeys, which would soon be put into the ovens to bake. Heath was counting out glasses and silverware.

"Aunt Claire," Heidi said plaintively, "can we go outside? It's not raining no more."

"Anymore," Claire corrected, "And, no, you can't, because it's way too muddy right now."

"Then can you and Mr. Fearsome play hide-and-seek with us?" Henry asked.

"I'm afraid not." Claire wished she did not have to disappoint them. "I've got way too much work to do to get ready for the Thanksgiving feast this afternoon. But I'll tell you what I can do for you two. I'll put your favorite video on for you."

The twins looked less than thrilled. Claire understood. They were attuned to the energy in the air. They wanted to be part of it. And couldn't be, at least not on the level they would have liked, had it been a more low-key, strictly family affair.

Vowing to make it up to them later, Claire led them into the family room and set up the television for them. She returned to the kitchen. Buzz Aberg walked in just as Heath said, "How many place settings did we need again?"

When Claire told him, they realized they were five short. And that party rental place where she'd gotten the china and crystal for the event was not open today.

"What do you want me to do?" Heath asked.

My hero, Claire thought with a sigh.

"Claire." Mr. Finglestein came in the door, before she could answer. "Bad news. That next wave of rain and the drop in temperature? The weather reports all predict it to be coming in around four-thirty this afternoon now, instead of seven."

Which meant she couldn't have the tables on the lawn, as she had planned. "We'll have to set up inside then."

"How?" Mrs. Finglestein asked.

Claire walked out into the front hall. Heath, Buzz and Mr. Finglestein all followed.

She heard a giggle, saw a flash of color and spotted one of the twins running up the stairs, and disappearing around the corner.

Oh, dear... They were getting wild.

The TV she'd left on had lost its viewers.

Claire switched it off and made a mental note to track them down as soon as possible and find *something* for them to do. Meanwhile, she had nine tables, six of them portable banquet tables, seating six each. The formal trestle table in the dining room sat eighteen. She sized up the available space on the first floor and tried to figure out how to make more. "I guess we'll have to move furniture."

An hour later, they had tables all over the downstairs. It was a far from perfect arrangement, but the best they could do under the circumstances. At least they'd guarantee dinner seating out of the rain for everyone. Claire just hoped the storm didn't knock out the electricity again, at least not until after the food was prepared.

She consulted Buzz—who had graciously helped move sofas and chairs out of the way—about the new arrangement. "Do you want a formal seating chart?"

He frowned. "We probably better. Otherwise, there might be some grumbling..."

As Claire went to get a notepad and pen to work on it, she saw another flash of movement crossing the floor, a shoe peeking out from beneath a coat tree crammed with garments. The twins were still playing hide-and-seek. Well, as long as it was keeping them happily occupied, she supposed it was okay.

Half an hour, and several sightings of mischief later, Claire had the seating arrangement completed to Buzz's satisfaction.

"The Red Sage really is a lovely place," he said.

"Thank you." Claire smiled. They moved through the large living room, toward the front porch, where they stepped out into the afternoon sunshine. The temperature was a balmy sixty-five. Still not a cloud in the sky. It would have been a perfect day to have the feast outside on the lawn. A perfect day for the twins to be playing outside, had it not still been so muddy.

Privately vowing once again to make it up to them, Claire switched back to ranch manager mode and informed Buzz, "I've arranged for everyone who requested it to have horses available tomorrow, so you can cover the ranch on horseback. We're bringing in dirt bikes and hiking guides for the others, weather permitting."

Buzz nodded. "It really is heaven out there," he reflected.

Claire looked toward the mountains in the distance, the rugged canyon and rolling, sage-dotted territory in between. "I've always thought it was heaven, too," she said warmly. "Or as close as you'll get to it, here on earth."

"Wow, IT SMELLS GOOD in here," Heath said, several hours later.

Claire smiled, pleased everything was going so well, despite the challenges of trying to be a mom and a businesswoman simultaneously. "And we haven't even put the sides in the ovens yet."

She looked at Heath, so glad he had volunteered to work with her on this. It gave her an inkling what their future might hold. "Are the twins still playing hide-and-seek?"

He chuckled. "Last I saw."

Last she had seen, too. "Which was…?"

"Not sure. Maybe half an hour ago?"

Claire glanced at her watch. She couldn't believe how time was flying. "I better find them. They should have had lunch, or at least a substantial snack, a while ago." She headed into the hall, where tables were now set with snowy-white tablecloths, autumn-hued runners and a careful mix of rented and Claire's own family china and silver service.

The downstairs rooms were quiet. So was the second floor. Fighting back a vague feeling of alarm, Claire picked up her pace. "Heidi?" she called. "Henry?"

There was no response of any kind.

Claire's heart kicked against her ribs. "Come out, come out, wherever you are!" she said.

There was still no answer. She retraced her steps, looking under beds, in closets, behind furniture and draperies. Again, nothing.

Claire sprinted back down the stairs.

Heath was in the kitchen, setting up the caterer-size chafing dishes that would keep food warm while it was being plated. "Did they come in here?" She couldn't keep the panic out of her voice.

He immediately stopped what he was doing. "I'll help you look."

"Heidi! Henry!" They made their way through the ranch house, looking high and low. With a sinking heart, Claire checked the mudroom, staring at the hooks and shoe rack where the twins' outdoor play clothing was stored. Both their jackets—the lightweight windbreakers and their heavier fall coats—were there. But their boots and school backpacks were gone.

"THIS IS ALL MY FAULT," Claire told Heath, as they set out on the section of trail they had opted to cover. The stretch she felt Heidi and Henry were most likely to traverse. If the kids didn't lose their sense of direction, that is. It was hard to know how accurate their inner radar was—they had never been out on the ranch alone.

Heath cast a glance at the increasingly gloomy afternoon sky. "We're going to find them," he vowed.

The double set of footprints had marched through the mud, away from the ranch house, only to completely disappear on the cedar-chip-strewn trail.

Fortunately, there were plenty of volunteers spreading out and yelling for Heidi and Henry.

All the adults, save Buzz Aberg's wife, who was watching over the dinner—had offered to traverse sections of path. Mr. and Mrs. Finglestein, who were intimately acquainted with the Red Sage trail system, were handing out flashlights, walkie-talkies, maps and flares.

The sheriff's department had been called in, along with Claire's neighbors. The worry was darkness, which would fall in another two hours, or sooner if the approaching storm hit before then.

Wind whipped up, sending leaves and dirt flying.

"I should never have attempted this," Claire told Heath miserably, as they scanned the landscape. She paused to use her field glasses, to no avail. "I should have known it was too much. That I wasn't paying enough attention to the twins."

"They've been doing fine," Heath argued gruffly.

She fought back another wave of panic. "Obviously not, or they wouldn't have run away."

Heath scowled as he topped another rise and eyed the sage-covered countryside with determination. "Maybe they didn't run away. Maybe they're just looking for something."

Taken aback, Claire blinked. "Such as?"

He turned, shrugged. "A way to make sense of everything that's happened the last year..." His husky voice dropped a notch and his eyes met hers. "All they've lost, all they have gained."

And suddenly Claire knew why the twins had come out here. And what Heidi and Henry hoped...wished...they would find.

LIGHTNING WAS FLASHING and thunder booming in the distance when Claire and Heath topped the ridge that was the highest point on the ranch. Like the answer to their prayers, they saw two curly blond heads huddled together in the brush. The twins were clinging together as rain began to pelt their small bodies.

"Heidi! Henry!" Claire shouted, aware that she had never felt more grateful for anything in her entire life.

The twins turned toward her. The next thing she knew they were running into her and Heath's arms.

"We came to heaven to see Mommy and Daddy…" Heidi sobbed, one of her arms wreathed around Claire's neck, the other around Heath's.

Holding on to Claire and Heath the same way, Henry hiccupped. "Only they w-w-wasn't here. Even though me and Heidi wished really really hard on our birthday candles that they *would* come and see us…"

"Mommy and Daddy want to see us so much. Don't they?" Heidi asked in a quavering voice, while Heath got on the walkie-talkie and told everyone their prayers had been answered—the twins had been found.

Henry nodded, seeming finally to understand as much as a four-year-old was capable of comprehending about life and death. "Mommy and Daddy just can't come and see us."

"That's right," Claire murmured, stroking their damp hair, realizing for the first time in her life that she was up to this challenge, because she had to be.

"Which is why your mommy and daddy asked me to take care of you, because they knew they had to go to heaven, and weren't going to be here anymore," she continued, re-assuring the twins gently.

"But they do love you and they're watching over you, every minute of every day." That was why she and Heath had come to find them so quickly, Claire figured. They'd had a little help from Liz-Beth and Sven in heaven above.

"Mr. Fearsome, too?" Henry asked, with hope in his eyes.

Heath nodded before Claire could react. And she knew his involvement wasn't just a financial one any longer. Heath had taken the kids into his heart as much as she had taken them into hers. And the love they all shared was turning them into "family."

"THANKS FOR FINDING US with Aunt Claire, Mr. Fearsome." Henry yawned, sleepily. It was several hours later, and the twins were ready for bed.

"We was really scared 'cause we were lost." Heidi stifled a big yawn in turn.

"Your aunt Claire and I were scared, too," Heath told the children solemnly, as he and Claire tucked them into bed. "Do you have any idea how upset we would be if anything ever happened to you?"

"Very upset?" Heidi guessed.

"Very, *very* upset," he declared emotionally. He hugged each of them in turn.

Claire hugged the twins, too. "So don't ever run off like that again, okay? Promise me!"

"Okay," Henry agreed.

"We won't," his sister added, struggling to hold her eyes open.

Claire and Heath sat with them until they fell asleep, then eased from the room.

Outside it was raining like crazy. The temperature had dropped to the low fifties. The ranch house was warm and cozy, and still smelled of the many good things that had been cooked and served for dinner.

Across the yard, the cottages were all lit up within, creating a tableau cozy enough to inspire a Kincaid painting.

Thanks to the voluntary efforts of their guests, there were no more tables to clear or dishes to wash. Even the soiled linens had all been bundled up and carted to the laundry room. Claire was glad she and Heath had the rest of the evening to themselves for some much deserved time alone.

Knowing that what was in her heart had to be said, even

if now wasn't the ideal time, Claire switched on the washing machine and turned to him. "When the kids said they needed you to protect them during the storm, they weren't the only ones," she said frankly.

She searched his eyes. "You've done so much for me the past few weeks, helping out with the kids and the business, being so supportive regarding my feelings about the guest ranch, even though I know that, as banker and trust executor, you still have reservations about how this will all pan out. I just want you to know..." Claire paused, took a deep breath. "I couldn't have gotten through today without you."

Chapter Fourteen

Guilt slammed into Heath's chest with the force of a truck.

He doubted Claire would think he was *supportive* if she knew the fail-safe measures he had been taking. Measures that looked increasingly as if they were going to be necessary to implement if she wanted to maintain the business she and her late sister and brother-in-law had worked so hard to start.

"And there's something else," Claire continued, slipping into his arms. "Something even more important." She pressed her soft body against him. "I don't just desire you, Heath, or want you as a friend—I want a relationship with you…the kind that lasts for years and years."

Her throaty confession caught him by surprise. It wasn't that he didn't suspect how she felt; he did. He'd known by the way she looked at him sometimes, the way she touched him, kissed him and made love with him what they had going with each other.

It was the real thing.

Real enough to withstand learning the truth about how he had been attempting to protect her fiscally, without her knowledge?

Seeing his hesitation, Claire put up a staying hand and

ducked her head shyly. "You don't have to say anything. I know it's too soon for us to be talking like this."

Feelings surged inside him. Loving the way she felt against him, so warm and soft and womanly, he gathered her closer still. Gazing into her eyes, he did what he rarely did—confessed what was in the deepest regions of his heart. "I want an exclusive relationship with you, too, Claire, more than anything." And he kissed her with all the passion he felt.

When at last they came up for air, Claire paused, wet her lips. She seemed to know instinctively there was still something standing between them, keeping them apart. Figuring now was not the time to confess anything relating to business, especially something likely to cause an argument, Heath grinned.

"This wasn't how I envisioned the moment we'd decide to make our arrangement a more permanent one. I figured at the very least there'd be candlelight. A romantic dinner. A walk beneath a starry sky."

"Not a clandestine tryst in the laundry room, at the end of one of the most grueling Thanksgiving Days ever?"

Knowing he wanted Claire in a way he'd never wanted any woman before, he drawled, "The holiday had its perks."

Her cheeks warmed with a self-conscious blush. "Such as?"

"Seeing you in the kitchen this morning, all flushed and pretty, commanding everything going on with such aplomb."

She looked at him with gratitude and stated fervently, "I'm really glad you were by my side when we found the kids."

So was Heath—the experience had made him realize how much Claire and the twins needed him, and how much he wanted to be there for them. He linked hands with her, folding her smaller, more delicate palm into his. "I also liked being with you when we tucked them in tonight. Not to mention having Thanksgiving dinner with you and the kids and everyone else, and enjoying what was a truly incredible holiday meal, despite all the calamities."

Claire pressed her face against his shoulder and relaxed against him, letting out a contented sigh. "Amazing how well that meal came off, considering."

Luckily for them, Heath thought, Buzz Aberg's wife was a veteran of many a holiday meal and knew just how to slow things down, and then speed 'em up to feed the hungry crew.

"We have a lot to be thankful for," Claire murmured.

"Yes, we do. Especially…" Heath kicked the door shut behind them and drew her close yet again "…this."

The laundry room was not the place Claire would have chosen to make love with Heath, but the moment his arms were around her and his mouth was on hers, she knew they'd never make it to her bed. Not when she needed and wanted him this badly.

The first contact of tongue to tongue was so electric she moaned. Gripping her shoulders, he guided her back against the wall, using his body to pin her there. She reveled in the feel of his hard, strong form even as she went up on tiptoe to return his kiss.

They'd had so little time together, she really wanted to go slow with him tonight, make the moment last….

She slipped her hands under his sweater, running them up his back and down again, not stopping until she had his buttocks cupped in her palms. He kissed her slowly at first, then harder, deeper, until she was using sultry thrusts of her tongue and the sweet suction of her lips to drive him crazy, too.

Without breaking the kiss, he reached beneath her skirt,

divesting her of panty hose and the tiny triangle of silk she wore. Then he knelt before her, and with light, sure strokes of his hands, convinced her to part her legs for him.

"Tell me you want me," he murmured.

Wanting him didn't begin to cover it. She moistened her lips as he discovered the sweetness within, using mouth and hands and tongue. "I want you."

He continued the tantalizing love play until his fingers were wet with her essence. Head falling back, she arched against him, letting him explore the delicate folds to his heart's content. Pleasure swept through her, until she was deliciously aroused, unable to stand it a second longer.

"Heath…" She caught his head with her hands and looked down at him.

He grinned up at her with sheer male appreciation, slid back up to take her mouth in a seductive mating dance, thrusting his hands beneath her blouse. Unhooking her bra, he palmed her breasts and captured the sweet globes in his hands.

She tugged off his sweater. Her palms glided around him, massaging the muscled contours on either side of his spine, then, lower, the sexy curve of his buttocks, through the fine wool of his slacks. All the while, she kissed him, happy to take her time as he cupped the full weight of her breasts with his palms, flicking the nipples with his thumbs before bending to pay homage with his lips and tongue.

The next thing she knew her legs were wrapped around his waist. Shifting her upward, he moved to possess her. Heat, then need, filled her soul as he brought them together in the most provocative of ways.

Determined to give her the kind of thorough lovemaking she deserved, Heath drew out every caress, sweeping his hands down her body, kissing her until he felt her trembling. Then slowly, deliberately, their bodies melded in boneless pleasure. He surged forward, filling her to completion, and then there was no more prolonging the inevitable. They were climbing past barriers, seeking release, finding each other in the most intimate of ways.

Afterward, they clung together breathlessly.

And, in that moment, Heath knew the last thing he wanted was any secrets between them. Which meant that as soon as the weekend ended and the pressure was off, he would tell her everything he had in mind to preserve the twins' inheritance...and to ensure the prosperity of Claire's family legacy.

"YOU'RE TO BE congratulated," Buzz Aberg drawled Sunday afternoon when he strode into the ranch office to hand over all the keys and complete the checkout process for his group. "I can't remember when my family had such a great Thanksgiving weekend."

"Even with all the calamities the first day or so?" Claire asked with a laugh.

"Hey, what's a family holiday without a little drama?" He winked.

Even if it hadn't been his clan causing the ruckus, Claire thought. "And everyone pitching in," she added, serious now.

Buzz sobered, too. "How are the twins doing, by the way?"

"Better," she reflected, finally feeling as if she was getting a handle on this mothering business, after all. "They're still grieving the loss of their parents, of course, but it's as if something changed on Thursday, when they were out there all alone. As if they finally started to come to terms with the changes in their lives."

Changes no one could have foreseen, or wanted. "I think on some level they still know it's going to take a while, but they also know that Heath and I will be there to see them through it," she stated.

Buzz gave her the empathetic look of a fellow parent. "It's easy to see that they love you—and Heath—very much," he said gently.

Claire thought so, too.

Buzz glanced at the corner where all the toys were stowed. "Where are they this afternoon?"

Claire smiled. "On a playdate with preschool friends for the rest of the day." She and Heath both felt the change of scenery would do them good, so he had driven them into town for her. Their friends' parents were going to drive them back to the ranch after supper, so she could concentrate on her business. Speaking of which...

"Have you made a decision about whether or not to run a review of the ranch in *Southwestern Living?*" Claire asked.

Buzz gave her a thumbs-up. "I think it's such a great place to celebrate the holiday we're going to run it in the November issue next year."

Claire's heart sank. That was twelve months from now. She tried to play it cool, and not put Buzz, who had already gone out of his way to accommodate her, on the spot. "What about the Web site?" she asked cordially. "Can you post a review there now?"

"No. That won't go up until the issue the review is published in hits the newsstands."

Which would be way too late to help her drum up business right now, Claire realized in disappointment. So she would have to go back and work on Plan B. Get it nailed down before she talked to Heath at the bank on Tuesday. That gave her just a little over forty hours… She did her best to squelch a sigh.

Buzz continued, "You'll be pleased to know that the Red Sage is going to be given a five-star review, our highest. We'll be back out to take pictures of some of the more scenic places in the ranch, a few months prior to publication. So if that party barn of yours is up and running, by say…July, we'll be able to include that, too."

"That's great." Claire smiled, shook hands with him and walked him to the door.

As he exited, the Finglesteins walked in, to turn in their key. They were dressed in winter clothing geared for their destination, upstate New York. "Claire, once again, we can't tell you how much we enjoyed our stay," Mrs. Finglestein exclaimed.

"If that's the case," she said with a smile, prepared to call in every favor owed her, and then some, "perhaps there is something you can do for me…."

THE LAST OF THE GUESTS were driving out of the ranch when Heath drove in. Claire went out to meet him. She wound her arms around his neck, and they indulged in a kiss. "Alone at last." By her calculation, they had two hours to do whatever they pleased. She didn't intend to waste a second of it. Given the way he was kissing her, he didn't, either.

He kissed her ear, down the slope of her neck. "I was going to say 'your place or mine?' but since my place is still your place, at least for the moment…"

Claire laughed. Arm in arm, they started for the ranch house, only to have another vehicle pull up behind them. Claire paused as a familiar figure stepped out of her car.

Hating the interruption, but aware she still had a job to do as innkeeper, Claire walked toward the real-estate broker. "Ginger. What brings you back to the ranch?"

Ginger reached into her Mercedes and brought out a briefcase. "I'm here to see Heath."

Stunned, Claire turned to him.

Ignoring the question in Claire's eyes, Heath gave Ginger Haedrick a meaningful look. "This isn't a good time."

To his obvious frustration, she didn't take his none-too-subtle hint. "You asked me to put a rush on the information. I did. I'd like to at least give you the facts and figures now, since I worked most of the last two days putting it together for you. And, Claire, you should see this, too."

Heath's uncomfortable reaction caused Claire's suspicions to rise.

"As I said—" Heath began bluntly, making it clear he wanted Ginger to leave.

Not about to let that happen, without at least getting an idea as to what was going on, Claire held up a palm. "I'd like to hear what Ginger has to say. Let's go over to the ranch office." Where she could at least pretend to be in control of the situation.

When they were all seated, Ginger handed out two folders with her business logo on the cover. Inside, Claire was stunned to find photos of the various cottages, as well as the Red Sage ranch house and barn. They were the kind of pictures usually featured in realty company advertisements.

"As you can see, I've assigned a price to each of the surface improvements on the property," Ginger said. "I also looked up the mortgage on each building. So even if you were to pay a real-estate commission, you would still emerge with a nice profit, per building, assuming you got your asking price."

Claire worked to keep her voice even. "That's nice information to have, but I'm not selling the cottages."

Ginger's eyes widened. "That's not what Heath said..."

He stood, signaling the meeting was over. "Thank you for putting this together, Ginger. We'll be in touch." He walked her out while Claire stewed.

When he returned to the office, it was all Claire could do to maintain her composure. "You want to tell me what that was all about?" she demanded coolly.

Heath sat down, as if nothing were amiss. "First, I want to know how the final meeting with Buzz Aberg went."

Mirroring his oh-so-easy attitude, Claire perched on the edge of her desk, facing him. "*Southwestern Living* is giving the Red Sage a five-star review," she announced with pride. Then she added reluctantly, "Unfortunately the glowing summation won't be printed until next Thanksgiving."

"So it's good for the long term..."

"And lousy for the short term," Claire summed up, still feeling equal parts elated and discouraged. She studied his implacable expression, then noted, with dismay, "Which, obviously, you expected."

He gave her a level look. "I plan for every contingency, Claire. It's my job."

Hurt warred with indignation. "So you're what?" Unable to contain her skyrocketing emotions a second longer, she bounded off her desk and paced the room restlessly, fists balled at her sides. "Planning to sell the cottages out from under me?" She whirled to face him. "Or at least the half of the business owned by the trust for the twins?"

He stood slowly. "I had in mind putting one cottage on the market."

Unable to believe his gall, Claire sent him a withering glare. "Thanks for letting me know!" she said sweetly, unable to believe she had allowed herself to be so vulnerable with him. She had known all along how different they were.

"I wasn't going to do it without your knowledge."

"Did you plan on getting my consent?" she demanded heatedly.

Heath shrugged, refusing to back down. "I had hoped to." He enunciated the words clearly.

Feeling all the more devastated, she queried, "And if not…?"

He stepped closer and his low voice took on that uncompromising note she knew so well. "As I've explained, the trust must produce some income. It can't continue operating as it has for the past nine months. The loss you incurred hosting Buzz Aberg and his family puts your ledgers firmly in the red, not just for the month of November, but the current fiscal year, which—for your business—started in September." He took a deep breath before continuing. "We have to find a way to counter that, if you want to maintain the Red Sage pretty much as is. One way to do that is by selling off part of the assets, such as one of the cottages."

Claire shot daggers at him. "But you know how I feel—"

He held up a hand before he had a chance to protest further. "Just listen. That would still leave you with eleven cottages to rent out, until things turn around. Then, under terms I'm proposing, you could purchase the cottage back, if you so desired, or work a deal with the new owner to lease it out as well. Maybe as sort of a time-share."

Claire drew a shaky breath, her thoughts in turmoil. All

she knew for sure was that she had never felt so betrayed. "So you never really believed in me or my merit as a businesswoman, after all!" Had everything between them been an act on his part? she wondered. Worse, how had she ended up with a man who doubted her capability, and made it public knowledge that he felt that way?

"I believe you are a visionary," Heath said cautiously.

"Just not the kind of person who can successfully implement grand plans," Claire retorted, her voice tinged with bitterness.

Heath held his ground. "They are separate skill sets."

And he obviously considered her decidedly lacking in one of them!

Stung by his lack of respect, knowing without respect there could be no love, none that mattered, anyway, Claire moved closer. "Well, I'll tell you what hasn't been separate and should have been!" she fumed. "My feelings for you and the control you exercise over the trust for the twins and the future of the Red Sage Guest Ranch!"

Heath folded his arms across his chest. "You have to know I would never do anything to hurt you."

Claire wondered how she could have been foolish enough to imagine the two of them sharing a life together.

"Don't you get it?" she cried bitterly, as her dream of loving each other as equals shattered. "In undermining me this way, you already have."

"SO THE TWO OF YOU broke up?" Orrin Webb surmised the next day, in the staff room at the bank.

Heath exhaled, as the stone that was lodged in his chest grew heavier. "Looks like. Although we didn't actually get that far in our discussion. Claire kicked me off the property before I had a chance to finish talking with her."

She'd given him just enough time to pack his bags and head out. Instead of moving back into the cottage he had vacated for the overflow of guests, he'd found a motel room in town. And spent the night alternately missing Claire and being furious with her, for being so irrational yet again.

Heath's mentor shook his head. "You shouldn't have gone behind her back to get those appraisals."

"I needed to know the value of the cottages to see if the idea was even plausible."

Orrin plucked an apple Danish from the bakery tray. "She felt blindsided."

Frustration combined with the guilt that roiled in Heath's gut. "I was trying to help." In fact, he felt he should be commended for his actions, not censured.

The older banker poured coffee into a mug. "Maybe you're too close to the heirs of the trust to manage it properly."

Heath sipped his own coffee. His boss had clearly made the brew. It was hot, black and strong enough to stand a stick in. "That is the first thing we agree on today." Since he'd become involved with Claire, his professional detachment had disappeared. He'd viewed the entire situation way too personally, and for a while, anyway, that had hampered his ability to do his job.

"You still have a chance to salvage the situation."

Heath hoped so. A life without Claire and the twins was no life at all.

"CONSIDERABLY QUIETER here this morning than over the weekend," Mae noted Monday, when she came in to work.

Together, she and Claire headed to the first cottage to be cleaned that morning, the one nearest the ranch house.

"I guess Heath will be moving back in today, right? Now that the cottages are all emptied out."

Claire shook her head. "He moved out altogether."

"Heath moved out?" Mae asked with surprise, as they pushed the cleaning cart in the door.

Claire carried in fresh linens. "Yesterday."

"That sounds...ominous."

Claire knew she had to talk to someone. And since Mae was the closest thing she had these days to a mother, she confided everything that had transpired.

The older woman listened intently. "Hmm," she said when Claire had finished.

"What does that mean?" Claire demanded.

"Just thinking."

This was like pulling burrs out of a dog's coat. "About...?"

"You didn't seem to mind Heath's help reading the twins stories and putting them to bed at night. I don't recall you complaining when he sacrificed every moment of spare time he had last week to help you get ready, and then cater to Buzz Aberg and his family. In fact, I believe Heath logged way more hours than I did. Unpaid."

Heat crept into Claire's cheeks. "He offered to do that."

"And you accepted with nary a complaint. And yet whenever he's tried to help you in a monetary sense by asking you to consider offers from Wiley Higgins or the Wagner Group or Ginger Haedrick's realty, all you feel is insulted."

Claire stripped the sheets from the bed with a vengeance. "He should have respected my ability to run this guest ranch!"

Mae gathered up the linens from the bathroom, dumped them in the wheeled hamper. "Like you respected his abilities as a banker and trust manager to come up with creative financial solutions to what was clearly his problem as much as yours?"

Claire fell silent.

Mae patted her shoulder and continued gently, "All I'm saying is that it takes two to make a relationship work, and two to make it fail. You need to decide which side of the equation you're on. And then go from there."

CLAIRE THOUGHT ABOUT WHAT Mae had said the rest of the day, while she worked on her own solution to the lack of bookings. By evening, she had accomplished what had once seemed impossible. Tempering the vindication she felt was the loss of Heath in her life.

She knew in retrospect that Mae was right.

She had been far too hasty in giving Heath the boot.

Claire glanced at Liz-Beth's photo on her desk. "I know, little sis," she said softly. "I'm never going to get what you found with Sven if I won't swallow my pride."

And that was the first thing she intended to do the next morning. After the twins left for preschool.

Thankfully, the breakfast buffet at the Red Sage Tuesday morning was sparsely attended. Wiley Higgins, who was now scouting for oil on one of her neighbors' ranches, zipped in the moment she set the food and beverages out. Her only other guest at the moment was T. S. Sturgeon, who was putting the finishing touches on her novel. And after working all night, she was now sleeping. The novelist had requested a tray be delivered to her cottage later.

"Where's Mr. Fearsome?" Heidi asked, while she and her brother waited for the car pool to pick them up.

It wasn't the first time in the previous thirty-six hours the twins had mentioned Heath. To Claire, it seemed they did so at least twice an hour.

"Yeah," Henry chimed in, defiantly enunciating every word. "We want to say hi to him!"

Claire gulped around the knot in her throat. It was not too late to fix things between the two of them. It couldn't be. "Mr. Fearsome is not staying with us anymore," she explained to the twins, for what seemed like the millionth time since his departure.

"How come?" Henry demanded, as if by asking the same question repeatedly he'd eventually hear an answer he liked.

Because, like a fool, I told Heath I didn't want to see him anymore, and kicked him off the property, Claire thought.

Fortunately, she was going to see him this afternoon, because today was December first, and she had to go to the bank to talk to him about the twins' trust fund.

"Don't you want him to be our friend anymore?" Heidi asked.

That's just the problem, Claire thought, as a familiar vehicle drove up the lane and parked in front of the ranch house. *I do.*

The luxury sedan was followed by an equally familiar minivan.

Heath got out of the first vehicle, while the driver of that morning's preschool car pool waited patiently.

"Mr. Fearsome!" Ignoring their ride, backpacks banging at their sides, the twins raced out the door, down the steps and around the open car door. They barreled into Heath, engulfing him in exuberant hugs. "We missed you!"

"I missed you, too." His voice was husky with emotion, his eyes warm and tender. His clothing was totally professional, however, suggesting he was here on trust business and nothing more.

Pretending an inner cool she couldn't begin to feel, Claire instructed the kids to say goodbye to Heath, then went to strap them into their seats. She waited until the minivan had driven off, before turning back to him.

Her heart sank when she saw he already had his briefcase in his hand. Which could only mean one thing: he *was* here strictly on business.

Disappointment spiraled through her.

Yet she knew this was important, too. And needed to be dealt with, ASAP. Using politeness as a shield, she said, "There's no need for us to talk on the porch. Please come in." With a stiff smile on her face, she paused before the breakfast buffet. "Can I get you something?"

His attitude was equally formal. "No. Thank you."

Deciding the ranch house held far too many memories for a conversation of this ilk, Claire led Heath to the office. Which, as it turned out, held just as many memories. Of Heath striding in to meet with her…. Bending down to talk to the kids…. Taking off his suit coat, rolling up his sleeves, and fixing her broken fax machine…. Pulling her into his arms to deliver a hot, searing kiss—one of many they had shared over the last few weeks.

Shoving her emotions aside, she gestured for him to have a seat, and tried to compose herself while they got business out of the way. "I thought we had an appointment for later this morning in town…"

One that had been set up weeks ago, before she and Heath became romantically involved.

One neither of them had seen fit to reschedule or cancel, even with the recent turn of events.

Heath gave her a brief, officious look. "You do. But it's not going to be with me. I'm here to let you know that as of right now, I am no longer managing the twins' trust. That will be done by Orrin Webb, the branch manager and my boss."

This, Claire had not expected, although maybe she should have. Her heartbeat quickening, she tried to decipher what it all meant.

"I requested the management of the trust be reassigned," Heath explained.

Claire's anxiety rose. Ignoring the sudden wobbliness in her knees, she sat down behind her desk. "Why?"

His lips twisted ruefully. "Because I've become way too emotionally involved with the trust beneficiaries and their guardian."

A statement, Claire noted cautiously, that could be read any number of ways. Wary of jumping to conclusions, she inquired, "Is this going to be good or bad for me?"

The sexy smile she knew and loved flashed across his face. He lounged back in his chair, relaxing as the talk turned unerringly to business. "It'll be good for a couple of reasons. Orrin is incredibly experienced and a wiz at merging the practical and the sentimental, while maintaining a fiscally strong bottom line."

Claire tried not to notice how blue Heath's eyes looked in the morning light. Or think how much she wished she could dispense with all this and simply kiss him. "And second?" she asked, unable to do anything about the distinctly husky sound of her low voice.

Heath stood, taking command of the room and the conversation once again. "You and I will no longer have reason to disagree over the management of the trust, because if you accept my proposal, and I sincerely hope that you will..." he paused to remove some papers from his briefcase "...then your current financial problems will be over."

"Really," Claire said doubtfully, almost afraid to hope that everything could work out between them, after all.

He gazed into her eyes. "Really," he answered softly.

A terse but expectant silence fell between them. He handed her a written offer for the cottage he had been staying in before the Thanksgiving weekend. Claire studied the paper, and found the offer to be more than generous. It had his name on the contract as purchaser of the property.

"You'll notice it gives you first right of refusal in any future sale, and also the right to request that I not actually live in the dwelling." He paused to let her consider that, before continuing deferentially, "If that's the case, and the cottage is used only for rental purposes to ranch guests, as property owner I would get a percentage of the profits from that."

Claire adapted his businesslike attitude. "Sounds fair."

"The cash from the sale of the cottage would in turn give you the ten percent down payment for the low-interest small-business loan you need to turn the barn into a five-star party facility. Rental fees from that would more than put the Red Sage in the black from here on out." He then proceeded to further detail the specifics of his business proposal.

Claire leafed through the various agreements he had given her. Impressed, and more than a little overwhelmed, she murmured, "This plan is incredible. Add to that my deal with bird-watching groups in the East…"

Heath lifted a curious brow.

It was Claire's turn to shine. "Thanks to the video shot by the Finglesteins showcasing one hundred and twenty of the three hundred bird species that inhabit the ranch during the course of the year—and my willingness to discount room rates to groups—I've got reservations all the way through next summer. I had planned to present the news to you at the bank today."

His expression rueful, Heath stroked his jaw. Then his blue eyes brightened with admiration. "So you didn't need my help."

Now was the time, Claire thought, to go for it. Put her feelings on the line and see what happened. Her heart pounding, she rose from her chair and walked around her desk to do what she hadn't done before—meet him halfway. "I wouldn't say that."

Heath regarded her with a look that brought forth a spate of feelings.

Swallowing the last of her pride, she slipped her arms about his neck. "I do need you, Heath," she confessed, pressing her body against his. "And I want you in my life." She kissed him fervently, letting all her feelings show.

Heath stroked a hand through her hair and tilted her face up to his. "I need and want you, too, Claire. So much…"

They kissed again, even more meaningfully.

When the passionate kiss finally drew to a halt, Claire gazed into his eyes. "And I'm sorry about the way I reacted to the news of what you were trying to do." She swallowed. "I thought to be successful, to earn your respect, I had to succeed entirely on my own, at least from a management perspective. I see now that isn't true. Garnering potential solutions to my problems from other sources is a part of my job, not the sign of weakness I deemed it to be."

Heath accepted her apology even as he offered up one of his own. "You had a right to be angry. I went behind your back."

Claire shook her head, fingering the knot of his tie. "Only because I was so unreceptive to the help you were trying to give me."

He slid a hand beneath her chin and tilted her face up to his again. As their eyes met, he confessed, "I should have trusted that you would figure out how to make your dreams a reality, given a little more time."

Happiness bubbled through her. Claire splayed her hands across his chest and felt the strong, reassuring beat of his heart. "Maybe in the future we should accept that we'll never be as strong alone as we are together."

Heath flashed her a victorious grin. "You're right about that."

They paused for another long, sustaining kiss. "I love you, Claire, with all my heart," he whispered in her ear.

She nestled against him as she heard the words she had longed to hear, and at last, all her dreams began to come true. "I love you, too, Heath." More than she had ever thought possible.

Chapter Fifteen

Thanksgiving, the following year...

"Mr. Fearsome, Mr. Fearsome, I've got the ring pillow!" Henry raced to catch up with Heath.

"And I've got the basket of flowers!" Heidi said, dashing along at her brother's side.

Heath knelt and looked into the faces of the two children he had come to love so much. "A finer flower girl and ring bearer could not be found," he told the twins with a solemnity befitting the occasion.

Henry tugged on the bow tie of his child-size tuxedo, until it was completely askew. "I'm going to do my part real good," he declared.

"Me, too. I'm going to put flowers everywhere!" Heidi promised, touching the floral wreath in her hair and then the satin bow on her pretty organza dress.

Heath straightened the boy's bow tie again, while Henry presented the velvet pillow he'd been carrying since they arrived at the Summit, Texas, community chapel. "See the rings? They're shiny and new!"

"Yes, they certainly are," Heath agreed.

Like his feelings for Claire.

Slightly over a year had passed since they had met. So much had changed, and so much had stayed the same. Thanks to the interior renovation of the Red Sage party barn, reservations for the ranch were up two hundred percent. Bird-watchers from all over the country were now flocking to the ranch to view the three hundred species of birds. The just-published review from *Southwestern Living* magazine had increased interest and bookings, to the point Claire was looking at expanding again, with more cottages and an additional area of primitive campgrounds, for those interested in roughing it.

"Can we walk up there?" Heidi pointed to the ribbon-and-flower-bedecked aisle, where the wedding vows would be spoken.

"Not yet," Heath said. "We have to wait for Aunt Claire to come out of there." He pointed to the anteroom where Claire and her bridesmaids were still dressing.

Heidi's lower lip shot out. "I want to see her!" she declared.

"Me, too!" Henry hopped up and down on one foot.

Me, three, Heath said silently, since every second away from his bride-to-be was a second too long.

Telling himself to be patient, he glanced again at the pews. Approximately half the guests had arrived....

For the sake of tradition, he was about to try to stall the twins—yet again—when the door opened and a slender hand beckoned. The twins rushed forward. "Aunt Claire!" They disappeared through the door.

Heath looked after them wistfully, wishing he, too, could get a glimpse of the beautiful woman inside.

The hand beckoned once again.

His spirits rose.

Heidi stuck her head out the door. "Come on, Mr. Fearsome! Aunt Claire says it's okay!"

He didn't have to be invited twice. Hands in his pockets, he sauntered in.

All too willing to grant the family-to-be a little privacy, the bridesmaids slipped out.

The door shut.

The four of them were alone, and Claire was a vision in white. Delicate, ethereal, strong, sexy, smart. In short, everything he had ever wanted in a woman and a wife.

She looked him up and down, her smile spreading. "Nice." Her eyes twinkled as she continued perusing him in a fashion that promised a very compelling wedding night. "Very nice."

Heart racing, Heath took her in his arms. "I could say the same about you," he murmured appreciatively.

Always beautiful, Claire looked spectacular today. She had a wreath like Heidi's in her hair, with a short veil attached. Her wedding dress was made of white satin, and left most of her shoulders and arms bare. It hugged her midriff tightly before flowing out at her waist.

"What about us, Aunt Claire?" Heidi demanded for herself and her brother.

"You look very nice, too," Heath and Claire said in unison.

The door opened once again. Mae Lefman stood there. She smiled at Claire and Heath. "I'll take these two off your hands for a few minutes."

Heidi and Henry raced toward their favorite neighbor and babysitter. "Bye, Aunt Claire! Bye, Mr. Fearsome!"

"Think they'll ever start calling me uncle?" Heath asked,

when the door shut yet again and he and Claire were alone at last.

Looking deep into his eyes, Claire murmured, "Eventually. Although…" she paused to straighten Heath's bow tie with the kind of wifely devotion he was already savoring "…I think their mispronunciation of your last name is kind of cute."

Heath chuckled. "I admit I'm kind of attached to it, too."

They kissed again.

When they drew apart, Claire left her arms around his neck and said, "I want you to know, Mr. Fearsome, that today is the best day of my life."

"So far," Heath qualified, tracing her silky lower lip with the pad of his thumb. "We've got many, many more to come."

"Yes," Claire echoed softly, "we do."

That sentiment was repeated in their wedding ceremony.

And in the wedding reception and Thanksgiving dinner that followed at the Red Sage Guest Ranch party barn. The space had been turned into a high-ceilinged banquet hall complete with an amazing dance floor, crystal chandeliers and polished oak walls. When everyone was seated at linen-draped tables, Heath stood and raised his elegant crystal glass in a toast. "To everyone here and all we have to be thankful for," he proposed, "on this Thanksgiving Day." Which was so much…

"Here, here," the guests murmured in response.

"Kiss Aunt Claire again, Mr. Fearsome!" Henry yelled enthusiastically, above the clink of glasses.

"Yeah, kiss her!" Heidi insisted, clapping her hands together.

Amid smiles and murmurs of approval, Heath happily complied.

* * * * *

*Do you love stories about instant families?
Look for the next book in
Cathy Gillen Thacker's MADE IN TEXAS miniseries,
A BABY IN THE BUNKHOUSE,
coming December 2008,
only from Harlequin American Romance!*

Here's a sneak peek at
THE CEO'S CHRISTMAS PROPOSITION,
the first in USA TODAY *bestselling author*
Merline Lovelace's HOLIDAYS ABROAD *trilogy,*
coming in November 2008.

American Devon McShay is about to get the Christmas surprise of a lifetime when she meets her new client, sexy billionaire Caleb Logan, for the very first time.

Silhouette Desire

Available November 2008

Her breath whistled out in a sigh of relief when he exited Customs. Devon recognized him right away from the newspaper and magazine articles her friend and partner Sabrina had looked up during her frantic prep work.

Caleb John Logan, Jr. Thirty-one. Six-two. With jet-black hair, laser-blue eyes and a linebacker's shoulders under his charcoal-gray cashmere overcoat. His jaw-dropping good looks didn't score him any points with Devon. She'd learned the hard way not to trust handsome heartbreakers like Cal Logan.

But he was a client. An important one. And she was willing to give someone who'd served a hitch in the marines before earning a B.S. from the University of Oregon, an MBA from Stanford and his first million at the ripe old age of twenty-six the benefit of the doubt.

Right up until he spotted the hot-pink pashmina, that is.

Devon knew the flash of color was more visible than the sign she held up with his name on it. So she wasn't surprised when Logan picked her out of the crowd and cut in her direction. She'd just plastered on her best businesswoman smile when he whipped an arm around her waist. The next moment she was sprawled against his cashmere-covered chest.

"Hello, brown eyes."

Swooping down, he covered her mouth with his.

Sheer astonishment kept Devon rooted to the spot for a few seconds while her mind whirled chaotically. Her first thought was that her client had downed a few too many drinks during the long flight. Her second, that he'd mistaken the kind of escort and consulting services her company provided. Her third shoved everything else out of her head.

The man could kiss!

His mouth moved over hers with a skill that ignited sparks at a half dozen flash points throughout her body. Devon hadn't experienced that kind of spontaneous combustion in a while. A *long* while.

The sparks were still popping when she pushed off his chest, only now they fueled a flush of anger.

"Do you always greet women you don't know with a lip-lock, Mr. Logan?"

A smile crinkled the skin at the corners of his eyes. "As a matter of fact, I don't. That was from Don."

"Huh?"

"He said he owed you one from New Year's Eve two years ago and made me promise to deliver it."

She stared up at him in total incomprehension. Logan hooked a brow and attempted to prompt a nonexistent memory.

"He abandoned you at the Waldorf. Five minutes before midnight. To deliver twins."

"I don't have a clue who or what you're…"

Understanding burst like a water balloon.

"Wait a sec. Are you talking about Sabrina's old boyfriend? Your buddy, who's now an ob-gyn doc?"

It was Logan's turn to look startled. He recovered faster than Devon had, though. His smile widened into a rueful grin.

"I take it you're not Sabrina Russo."

"No, Mr. Logan, I am *not*."

* * * * *

Be sure to look for
THE CEO'S CHRISTMAS PROPOSITION
by Merline Lovelace.
Available in November 2008 wherever books are sold,
including most bookstores, supermarkets, drugstores
and discount stores.

Silhouette®
Romantic
SUSPENSE

Sparked by Danger, Fueled by Passion.

Lindsay McKenna
Susan Grant

Mission: Christmas

Celebrate the holidays with a pair
of military heroines and their daring men
in two romantic, adventurous stories
from these bestselling authors.

Featuring:

"The Christmas Wild Bunch"
by *USA TODAY* bestselling author
Lindsay McKenna
and

"Snowbound with a Prince"
by *New York Times* bestselling author
Susan Grant

Available November wherever books are sold.

REQUEST YOUR FREE BOOKS!
2 FREE NOVELS PLUS 2
FREE GIFTS!

Love, Home & Happiness!

YES! Please send me 2 FREE Harlequin® American Romance® novels and my 2 FREE gifts (gifts are worth about $10). After receiving them, if I don't wish to receive any more books, I can return the shipping statement marked "cancel." If I don't cancel, I will receive 4 brand-new novels every month and be billed just $4.24 per book in the U.S. or $4.99 per book in Canada. That's a savings of close to 15% off the cover price! It's quite a bargain! Shipping and handling is just 25¢ per book, along with any applicable taxes.* I understand that accepting the 2 free books and gifts places me under no obligation to buy anything. I can always return a shipment and cancel at any time. Even if I never buy another book from Harlequin, the two free books and gifts are mine to keep forever.

154 HDN EEZK 354 HDN EEZV

Name _____ (PLEASE PRINT) _____

Address _____ Apt. # _____

City _____ State/Prov. _____ Zip/Postal Code _____

Signature (if under 18, a parent or guardian must sign)

Mail to the **Harlequin Reader Service:**
IN U.S.A.: P.O. Box 1867, Buffalo, NY 14240-1867
IN CANADA: P.O. Box 609, Fort Erie, Ontario L2A 5X3

Not valid to current subscribers of Harlequin® American Romance® books.

Want to try two free books from another line?
Call 1-800-873-8635 or visit www.morefreebooks.com.

* Terms and prices subject to change without notice. N.Y. residents add applicable sales tax. Canadian residents will be charged applicable provincial taxes and GST. Offer not valid in Quebec. This offer is limited to one order per household. All orders subject to approval. Credit or debit balances in a customer's account(s) may be offset by any other outstanding balance owed by or to the customer. Please allow 4 to 6 weeks for delivery. Offer available while quantities last.

Your Privacy: Harlequin is committed to protecting your privacy. Our Privacy Policy is available online at www.eHarlequin.com or upon request from the Reader Service. From time to time we make our lists of customers available to reputable third parties who may have a product or service of interest to you. If you would prefer we not share your name and address, please check here. ☐

HAR08R2

Celebrate the joy of the holiday season with four heartwarming romances by acclaimed authors!

THE CHRISTMAS COLLECTION

Wanted: Christmas Mommy by JUDY CHRISTENBERRY

The Brands Who Came for Christmas by MAGGIE SHAYNE

All I Want for Christmas by GINA WILKINS

What She Wants for Christmas by JANICE KAY JOHNSON

Four Christmas novels… yours to enjoy in November 2008!

Available wherever books are sold, including most bookstores, supermarkets, discount stores and drugstores.

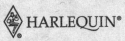

HARLEQUIN®

American ★ Romance®

LAURA MARIE ALTOM
A Daddy for Christmas

THE STATE OF PARENTHOOD

Single mom Jesse Cummings is struggling
to run her Oklahoma ranch and raise her
two little girls after the death of her husband.
Then on Christmas Eve, a miracle strolls onto
her land in the form of tall, handsome bull
rider Gage Moore. He doesn't plan on staying,
but in the season of miracles, anything
can happen....

*Available November
wherever books are sold.*

LOVE, HOME & HAPPINESS

www.eHarlequin.com   HAR75237

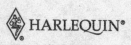

HARLEQUIN®

American ★ Romance®

COMING NEXT MONTH

#1233 A DADDY FOR CHRISTMAS by Laura Marie Altom
The State of Parenthood
Single mom Jesse Cummings is struggling to run her Oklahoma ranch and raise her two little girls. Then a miracle strolls onto her land in the form of a tall, handsome Texan. Gage Moore has his own troubles, so he doesn't plan on staying. But in the season of miracles, anything can happen....

#1234 THE CHRISTMAS COWBOY by Judy Christenberry
The Lazy L Ranch
Hank Ledbetter isn't the type of cowboy to settle down and raise a family. So when his grandfather orders him to give private riding lessons to Andrea Jacobs—a woman so *not* his type—he's bowled over by his attraction to the New York debutante. Andrea has another man in her life...but Hank's determined to be the only man kissing her this Christmas!

#1235 MISTLETOE BABY by Tanya Michaels
4 Seasons in Mistletoe
Rachel and David Waide want nothing more than to have a child. But after years of trying they are growing apart. Then Rachel discovers she is—at long last—pregnant! Now the two have to work their way back and remember all the love they used to share. Luckily, they'll receive a little help—in the form of a wedding, and the magic of Christmas.

#1236 THE COWBOY AND THE ANGEL by Marin Thomas
In his cowboy gear, Duke Dalton stands out in a crowd in downtown Detroit. He's there to set up his business, but some runaway kids are bunking in his warehouse. They need a Christmas angel—Renée Sweeney. And though Renée will do what she can to help the children, she wants nothing to do with Duke!

www.eHarlequin.com